It was going to be the best—
and the worst—sleepover ever.

Lexie looked at me with a wicked smile on her face. "You want to get rid of Samantha, right?"

"I guess," I said cautiously.

Lexie glanced over at Samantha, who was now in the middle of Cindy's tight little clique. "Between now and tonight we'll come up with a surefire plan to make her want to go home."

"That doesn't seem too nice," Kaitlin said.

Lexie rolled her eyes. "You think she's nice to us? Look at the way she talks to Emily. Look at the way she's always bragging. And if we have to put up with her much longer, we'll all be doing aerobics until we drop."

"So what will we do?" I asked.

Lexie shrugged. "You know her better than I do. What does she hate most in the world?"

"Me!" I said with a laugh. Then I shook my head. "It's no use. I don't know what she hates or what she's scared of."

"Then it will have to be trial and error," Lexie said. "If we keep at it all night, one thing will have to work and by morning she'll be begging to go home to L.A."

Check out the sleepover games in the back of this book!

TGIF!

#1 Sleepover Madness

#2 Friday Night Fright

#3 Four's a Crowd

TGIF!

Four's a Crowd

JANET QUIN-HARKIN

A MINSTREL®
BOOK

Published by POCKET BOOKS
New York   London   Toronto   Sydney   Tokyo   Singapore

A MINSTREL PAPERBACK *Original*

A Minstrel Book published by
POCKET BOOKS, a division of Simon & Schuster Inc.
1230 Avenue of the Americas, New York, NY 10020

Produced by Daniel Weiss Associates, Inc., New York

ISBN: 0-671-51019-3

First Minstrel Books printing November 1995

10 9 8 7 6 5 4 3 2 1

A MINSTREL BOOK and colophon are
registered trademarks of Simon & Schuster Inc.

Printed in the U.S.A.

ONE

"Okay. That's it. I quit," Lexie Taylor said dramatically as she opened the door at the end of the sixth-grade hall and peered out at the rain.

My other best friend, Kaitlin Durham, and I exchanged knowing looks. Lexie could be very dramatic at times. Maybe it's because her mother is an actress.

"Good, Lexie," I said. "'That's it and I quit.' It rhymes. Very creative."

"You're a poet and you don't know it," Kaitlin added with a grin.

Lexie turned around and glared at us. "Don't try to cheer me up when I'm in a bad mood," she growled. "I'm always grouchy when it rains."

"What are you quitting, Lexie?" Kaitlin asked as we got our lunches out of our lockers. "Mr. Meany's gym class?"

We had just finished one of Mr. Meany's aerobic torture sessions that left us crawling to the locker rooms, exhausted. Mr. Meany is our PE teacher. Meany by name, meany by nature, Lexie says. She's always coming up with funny things like that.

1

Lexie is my dramatic, funny friend. Kaitlin is more serious and shy and I am . . . I'm just plain old Emily Delgado—the chubby one with glasses. If that doesn't sound too exciting, I'm sorry. I'm working on it.

Lexie, Kaitlin, and I have been friends since we met in September as new sixth graders at Sonoma Middle School. It was Mr. Meany who really brought us together. He picked on all three of us from the first day of the school year. We'd probably still be his least favorite people if we hadn't gotten to know him better on Halloween night when we thought he'd turned into a werewolf. Actually, he was playing the role of a scientist who turns into a werewolf as part of a murder mystery weekend, but we didn't know it at the time. Now he's nicer, but his PE classes are still torture.

Lexie sighed and slammed her locker door. "I'd do anything to get out of gym class. Mr. M. never buys my excuses, though. Remember how he laughed when I told him I'd given my PE uniform to the homeless clothing drive?"

She turned to me. "You're the Einstein of Sonoma Middle School," she said. "How come you haven't come up with a brilliant plan to get us out of gym?"

I shrugged and didn't say anything. I hate it when my friends tease me about my great brain. I'm in all gifted classes, so I suppose I am kind of smart, but I'm certainly no second Einstein.

"I wasn't actually talking about Mr. Meany's class, though," Lexie went on. "I was thinking about quitting school."

"School?" Kaitlin demanded, looking at me again.

"You can't quit middle school," she said. "We're stuck here for two and a half more years and then four whole years of high school. I'm sure Emily the math whiz will tell you that's six years until we graduate."

"And there really aren't too many high-paying jobs for eleven-year-olds," I added. "You don't want to spend your life as a baby-sitter, do you?"

"You guys think I'm kidding," Lexie said. "I've had it up to here with this school. Not only do we have Meany torture sessions, but it rains every day, too."

Kaitlin and I started to laugh. "Lexie, I don't think you can blame school for the rain," I said. "Last time I looked, I didn't see 'rain' penciled in on the schedule for this week."

"Very funny," Lexie growled, still not ready to snap out of her bad mood for us. "I do realize the school can't make it rain. But they could do something about where we eat lunch. Not having a cafeteria is really primitive."

"We have a cafeteria," I interrupted. "It just happens to hold about ten people."

"They expect it always to be sunny," Kaitlin said. "That's why there are all those benches outside."

"And what happens when it rains all winter?" Lexie demanded angrily. "We'll have to eat lunch crammed into that stuffy gym with four hundred screaming kids every day. And Pee Wee Pugh throwing empty chip packets down the back of my neck is too much."

I should explain that Pee Wee Pugh is a giant sixth grader with a brain the size of a pea. His main hobby,

3

besides football, is making dumb animal noises with his friends and teasing girls, especially me and my friends. He and I went to the same elementary school and he's always loved giving me a hard time. Recently, though, I've been giving him a hard time back.

"Don't talk about chips," Kaitlin said. "You're making me hungry, and I know I've got another turkey-breast-and-sprout sandwich. My mother, the health-food nut, made my lunch. Your grandmother didn't happen to bake anything, did she, Emily?"

"Not recently," I said. "In fact, I haven't been over to her place since it started raining." My grandmother lives in a pretty white cottage on our ranch. We live way out of town in the middle of wine country. Sonoma, California, where we go to school, is famous for its vineyards, but we don't grow grapes ourselves. My mother breeds miniature horses and pygmy goats. My dad used to breed full-size horses, but after the divorce he moved out and took his horses with him. My new stepfather works in a winery, which isn't nearly as exciting. That's probably because he's not such an exciting person. He's boring, in fact. I still can't understand why my mother married him.

Well, enough about my problems. I try to stop at my grandmother's house on my way home from school every day. She is the world's best cook. Not only does she cook great Mexican food, she cooks great Anglo food too . . . and Chinese, and everything else. Both my mom's and dad's families came here from Mexico a long time ago.

"Oh, well," Lexie said, "I guess we have to go face

the zoo if we want to eat lunch." She started down the hall to the gym.

"I don't think my legs will walk that far," Kaitlin said. "Those aerobics exercises today were killers."

"I agree," I said. "By the end of class, my legs felt as if they'd turned to jelly."

"You'd think Mr. Meany would be nicer to us," Lexie said thoughtfully. "After all, we know that he's scared of snakes," she said triumphantly. "We found that out when we discovered that Mr. Meany *wasn't* a werewolf."

"He is nice to us now," I said. "He doesn't keep watching us out of the corner of his eye with that suspicious look anymore. He even kids around with us sometimes, and he does have a very cute smile. . . ." I stopped there, feeling myself starting to blush. I didn't want my friends to find out that I had a monster crush on Mr. Meany. Actually it wasn't a monster crush, but it was definitely growing.

"And really blue eyes," Kaitlin added.

Lexie spluttered. "You two are something else," she said. "How can you have a crush on a slave driver?"

"You like him, too, Lexie—admit it," Kaitlin said, giving me a knowing grin. "You think he's a hunk. And he called you spunky."

"Okay, so he's a hunk. And he has been nice to us since we thought he was a werewolf. And he did say I was spunky. Then why hasn't he tried to make gym class easier for us?"

"I guess he really believes his program will make

5

us super fit," Kaitlin said thoughtfully. She always sees the good side of everyone. "You have to admit that he's the fittest person you know. He does the aerobics with us and he never gets tired."

"Super fit or super dead," Lexie growled. She paused at the gym door. "Oh, well, here goes nothing." She opened the door and we were hit with a great blast of sound.

"I just love peaceful lunches," Lexie complained as we fought our way through the crowd and found a spot against the wall at the far end of the gym.

"Just think," Kaitlin said, "only two more weeks and we'll be free. I can't wait for Christmas vacation."

"Me either," Lexie said. "Almost three weeks of goofing off, doing nothing, hanging out with you guys."

"And the holidays in the middle of it," Kaitlin finished for her. "Presents, food, staying up late. . . ."

I gave a big sigh. The other two heard it and looked at me.

"What's up, Emily?" Kaitlin asked.

"It's just that I am definitely *not* looking forward to this vacation," I said.

"Why not?" Lexie asked.

I couldn't understand why they were being so dumb. "I told you," I said. "My stepsister, Samantha, is coming to stay."

"I don't see what's wrong with that," Lexie said.

I made a face. "You haven't met her. To start with, her name's Samantha—doesn't that sound prissy?"

"She can't help what she's called, Em," Kaitlin said. "I'm not wild about Kaitlin, but I'm stuck with it."

"I know it's not her fault," I said. "The trouble is that it fits her. She acts just like a Samantha."

"I think it would be fun having a sister your own age to do stuff with," Lexie said thoughtfully. "I hate being an only child."

"And I hate being the baby," Kaitlin added. "My brother and sister always think they can boss me around. I think you're lucky, Emily. It's like getting a ready-made twin."

"You won't say that when you see her," I said. "She might only be six months older than me, but she looks like she's at least fourteen years old. And she acts like it, too. She talks to me as if I'm a stupid little kid. And she's such a snob."

"Cheer up, Emily," Kaitlin said brightly. "Maybe it won't be as bad as you think. You've only met her a couple of times, right? She might be nice when you get to know her."

I shook my head. "I'm sure she'll be worse when I get to know her. She was a total pain both times I met her."

"But they were kind of stressful occasions, Emily," Lexie said. "People act weird when they're under stress. I know I'd freak out if I had to watch my dad or my mom marrying someone else. And statistics show that divorce is always hardest on the kids."

"She's right," Kaitlin said. "I'm no expert when it comes to stuff like that, but Samantha might have been very upset at the wedding."

"What about me?" I blurted. "You think it was

easy for me to watch my mother getting married to a strange man? Especially a geek like Ed. But I tried hard to be nice. I wasn't rude like Samantha was."

My mind went back to the wedding. Samantha and I weren't exactly bridesmaids, because it was an informal wedding, but we were sort of attendants. My mother had selected dresses she thought were pretty. They were flowery cotton with big puffed sleeves and wide sashes. I thought they really were pretty until the day of the wedding. That was when Samantha showed up in a totally different dress. Instead of the puffed sleeves and the wide sash, hers was silky, sleeveless, and very grown up. She had her hair up, too, and she looked about ten years older than me.

"I see you got stuck with that disgusting dress," she said, looking at me with pity. "It's totally the wrong shape for someone who's overweight like you. You should have refused to wear it, like me."

Then she walked away, leaving me feeling like a pricked balloon. I'd felt pretty good until then. Now I felt fat and flowery and very young. All through the wedding people came up to Samantha and told her how grown up and pretty she looked. They said I looked nice, too, but I could tell they were just being kind. And then they all said the same thing. "Won't it be wonderful for you to have a big sister?" I wanted to yell that she was only six months older than me and we were actually in the same grade at school and I was in all higher classes than her. But I didn't want to spoil my mother's day. So I kept quiet and prayed for the wedding to end.

And everything was okay until now. I'd almost forgotten that Samantha even existed, or at least what a big pain she was. Now I remembered exactly what she was like. The way she kept on telling me that she lived in Los Angeles, "but almost Beverly Hills," and how she went to school with the children of celebrities. I felt my stomach turning into knots as I thought of it. Now I had a whole vacation of putdowns to look forward to.

TWO

How would I ever get through two weeks with Samantha?

"You guys will have to come over and visit all the time, or I'll never survive the vacation," I yelled, trying to make myself heard over the noise level in the gym.

"Of course we'll be over all the time," Lexie said. "We love playing with all the animals. You know we only come to see the animals, not you." Then she saw my sudden look of disappointment and dug me in the ribs. "Joke, Em. I was just kidding. Boy, you really are down today, aren't you? We'll plan lots of fun things to do over the vacation." Her face lit up. "Maybe we could take some riding lessons."

"Not on our horses," I said in horror. "They're only two feet high."

"I know that, dummy. I mean riding lessons on regular-size horses. My mother's been promising and promising for as long as I can remember."

"I'd love to do that, too," Kaitlin said.

"I used to ride a lot," I said. "Back when my father had horses."

"I didn't know your father had horses," Kaitlin said with excitement.

"Oh, yes. He used to breed Arabians. I rode them all the time."

The picture came back vividly into my mind. I saw my dad, big, strong, tanned, and laughing, his dark eyes flashing as he swung me up into the saddle on one of his big horses. "Going to make a champion of you, kiddo," he'd say.

"What happened to them?" Lexie interrupted my dream.

"He took them with him when he moved away," I said. "The ranch belonged to my mother's family, so he was the one who left."

"That's too bad," Lexie said. "It would have been fun to go riding every day. And you could have given Samantha the fiercest horse and it might have bolted with her. Then you could have been the one who galloped after her and saved her and you'd have been the hero."

"Yeah!" I said, enjoying this fantasy. Lexie always came up with great schemes for getting even with people.

"Hey, maybe we can persuade Mr. Meany to give us a unit on horseback riding instead of aerobics," Lexie went on. "Then you could be the star."

"Yeah, right." Kaitlin and I started laughing. "Can you see the school providing thirty horses? And I'll bet Mr. Meany can't even ride."

"Can you imagine Pee Wee Pugh on a horse?" Kaitlin said.

This made us laugh really loudly.

"Poor horse!" Lexie exclaimed. "It would take one of those giant workhorses to hold him."

"And if he fell off, it would make a huge crater in the ground," I added, looking around until I spotted Pee Wee and his friends from the football team, sitting on the bleachers not too far from us.

He must have known we were looking at him. "Hey, Delgado, what's so funny?" he growled, pointing a big finger at me.

I wanted to say, "You are, Pee Wee," but I didn't. No sense in stirring up more trouble. So I said, "Nothing, Pee Wee, just an intellectual joke you wouldn't understand."

"Then keep the noise down," he went on. "Some people are trying to eat lunch in peace in here." He turned to his friends and went back to blowing up and popping chip packets.

"You notice how he's really cooled it these days," Kaitlin said.

"Ever since we cooled him, you mean?" I asked with a wicked laugh.

We had caught Pee Wee trying to egg a house at Halloween and we'd thrown ice and cold water all over him. Since then, he made fun of us a lot less.

The bell rang and everyone ran for the doors at the same time. "One at a time, ladies and gentlemen, please," the lunch monitors called, but it didn't do much good. They had to jump on the bleachers to stop themselves from being trampled. Lexie, Kaitlin, and I wisely hung back and were almost the last to leave.

As we walked down the hall to our lockers, we

passed our homeroom teacher, Mrs. Bliese. She was tacking a piece of paper to the board in the main hall.

"Girls, come and give me a hand with this, please," she called when she saw us. "I can't hold this flyer and tack it up at the same time."

We walked over to help her.

"Holiday talent show," Lexie read.

"That's right. It's a school tradition every December. Any kind of talent is welcome. You don't have to be an expert—it's just for fun. And I hope you'll help persuade a lot of my students to be in it, because I'm coordinating it this year. I'd like my homeroom to be well represented."

"Okay, sure," we all said. We held the flyer while Mrs. Bliese put thumbtacks in.

"Thanks, girls. Put on your thinking caps about what you're going to do for the show," Mrs. Bliese said. She started to walk away, then paused and turned back to us. "Oh, and Lexie—no live animals, okay?"

We giggled as Mrs. Bliese hurried away and we kept on going to our lockers.

"She still hasn't recovered from that time you brought Norman to school," Kaitlin said. Norman is Lexie's pet snake. She'd used him as part of her Halloween costume and he'd escaped, freaking out more people than Mrs. Bliese.

"That's not fair," Lexie said. "I could have done a great act with Norman. It's very impressive when he wraps himself around my arm. And I could wave him near Mr. Meany . . ."

"Poor Mr. Meany. You know he hates snakes," I said.

"I could make him promise to cut the aerobics," Lexie suggested. "Why did Mrs. Bliese have to spoil my big chance?"

We reached our lockers. As usual, a ton of stuff fell out of Lexie's when she opened it. As usual, Kaitlin and I scrambled to help her pick everything up.

"We have to come up with something to do," Kaitlin said as she took books from her own neat locker. "We sort of agreed, didn't we?"

"But what?" I asked. "What talents do we have?"

"Kaitlin can dance," Lexie said. "All those years of studying ballet—she should be an expert by now. Maybe you could teach us a dance, KD."

She always calls Kaitlin KD, which I think is a neat name for her. But I was shaking my head violently. "No, thank you, I'm positively not dancing. Have you ever seen me dance? I'd die of embarrassment and Pee Wee would yell out horrible things from the audience."

"Okay, scrub the dancing," Lexie said. "What do you and I do well, Em? I'm great with snakes and you can ride and do math puzzles. Hardly the start of a great act."

"We're funny when we get together," I said. "We make each other laugh. Maybe we could make other people laugh."

"Do a skit, you mean?" Kaitlin asked.

"Yeah, we'd have to come up with something funny," Kaitlin said. "What's funny about our lives?"

"Nothing," I said. "Everything seems like one big tragedy to me—my stupid stepsister wrecking my vacation and Pee Wee always teasing me. Mr. Meany will make us so exhausted that we won't be able to move for the entire vacation anyway."

Lexie draped her arm around me. "Come on, Em. Start thinking about funny stuff. You'll feel better when you've got something to occupy your great brain. Now what is a good subject for a skit?"

"It has to be about school," Kaitlin said. "Something all the other kids will appreciate."

"A skit about the teachers," I suggested.

"Making the teachers look stupid, you mean?" Lexie giggled. "Okay, Em, come up with a story for it."

"I'm too tired to think right now," I said. "Mr. Meany has sucked out all my energy."

Lexie let out a whoop of delight. "I've got the best idea—you're going to love it. Let's make up a Christmas story—you know, like all the cartoons on TV."

"Like Scrooge, you mean?" Kaitlin asked. "I love that story."

"I was thinking more about those stories where the snow monster steals Christmas or the mean king stops people from having fun . . . something like that," Lexie went on. She was waving her arms like she always did when her brain was working faster than her mouth. "How about this—the whole town is getting ready for Christmas. The town is owned by the terrible Mr. Monster Meany and he makes everyone work in his factory until they have no energy left to enjoy Christmas. They are too tired to bake or wrap presents or chop down Christmas trees."

"What do they make in the factory?" Kaitlin asked. She likes to get details straight.

"I know," I yelled. "Aerobics gear for the U.S. market!"

"This is supposed to be long ago and far away," Lexie said, annoyed that I wasn't taking her seriously. "Okay, so we'll make him a mean king who wants all his subjects to be super fit. They have to go to fitness classes until they drop. . . ."

"I don't get it," Kaitlin said. "Are you going to ask Mr. Meany to be in it?"

"No, we'll dress up like Mr. Meany, or maybe we'll ask one of the guys in our homeroom to do it. That wouldn't be too hard. We need a warm-up suit like he always wears and we put on tan makeup and a blond wig and we blow the whistle a lot . . ."

"And you know what else we could do?" Kaitlin suggested. "We could have other people in the story be other teachers. Mrs. Bliese could be the lady who's too tired to straighten up her messy house. You know what a neatness freak she is . . . and our English teacher is too tired to speak clearly and precisely . . ."

"Excellent," Lexie said. "We can work on it when we come over to Emily's house on Friday." Lexie turned to me. "The sleepover is still on, isn't it?"

"Sure," I said.

"Great. Hurry up, Friday," Lexie said. "We are going to create a killer skit. We'll be the stars of the talent show. Maybe my mother can bring her agent and we'll be signed up right away for a major motion picture deal."

"Yeah, right," I said, and laughed.

"Okay, but even if that doesn't happen, it will be

16

fun watching the teachers' faces—especially Mr. Meany."

"I hope he won't be mad at us," Kaitlin said. "He might think we're being obnoxious again, just when we're getting along okay with him."

"I'll bet he'll love it. I'll bet he thinks it's funny," Lexie said confidently. "Oh, this is going to be so great! We get to make fun of all the teachers and they just have to sit there and they can't do a thing about it!" she yelled, dancing down the hallway and waving her arms over her head.

"Alexis Taylor!" Mr. Meany's voice echoed down the hallway.

Lexie spun around guiltily. I could feel myself blushing again as Mr. Meany came toward us with a knowing smile on his face. I couldn't help noticing how handsome he was when he wasn't yelling at us to keep on moving—kind of like Brad Pitt.

"What were you doing, inventing a new dance to put in the next aerobics class?" he asked, grinning at our embarrassment. I was wondering how much he'd overheard.

"Just letting off some extra energy, Mr. Meany," Lexie said. "You know how you always say that fit people have tons of energy?"

Mr. Meany was still smiling. "I'm glad you're so fit now, Lexie. But if you have all that energy left, we need to raise the level of the aerobics exercises. Tomorrow we'll double the number of repetitions."

He didn't wait to hear Lexie's answer. He went on his way down the hall, whistling to himself. From the first day of school, it had been a battle of wills between him and Lexie, and it looked like Mr. Meany was still winning.

"Just you wait for the talent show, Mr. Meany," Lexie muttered as she watched him go. "We'll see who gets the last laugh."

THREE

The school bus dropped me off at the end of our road. It was a long, long walk to the house in the pouring rain. Branches dripped water down my neck, and the wind whipped rain into my face. I was so wet, cold, and miserable that I decided I needed to stop at my grandmother's house. Five minutes with her always cheered me up. I hoped she had baked one of her special goodies today.

I opened the door to the kitchen and the warm smell of baking rushed to meet me. "Hi, Nana, it's me," I called from the doorway.

Nana was sitting at the table, reading the paper. She jumped up when she saw me.

"Emily, you look like a drowned rat," she said. "Let's get that wet jacket off you and then you'll come sit by the fire. I'll make you some hot tea."

I let her take off my rain jacket as if I was a little kid. "And I'll bet you could use a slice of my special chocolate cake, too," she said, smiling fondly at me.

I looked across at the counter, which was piled high with muffins and brownies and pies. "Is there a bake sale at church or something?" I asked.

"You never know when extra goodies will come in handy," Nana said mysteriously. She cut me a big slice of chocolate cake and put it down beside my herbal tea. "There," she said. "That will warm you up."

"Thanks, Nana. You're the best grandma in the world," I said.

"And you're my favorite granddaughter," she said with a laugh. This was our little joke, because I was her only granddaughter.

I ate in contented silence. Nana's big orange cat, Marmalade, came to rub against my legs and then jumped into my lap. The fire crackled. It was warm and cozy in Nana's house. Everything was just right.

"I suppose you'd better get on home now," Nana said. "I think your mother is waiting for you to get home and help her."

"With what?"

"She'll tell you herself," Nana said mysteriously.

"What, Nana? Tell me, please," I begged.

Nana laughed and put her fingers to her lips, as if she were zipping them up. "Take my big umbrella," she said.

I hurried home, sloshing along the muddy path that led from my grandmother's house to ours. My mother's minivan was parked outside the barn. I wished she had picked me up from the bus today. I guessed she drove to get Robbie from his school. Robbie is my seven-year-old brother. My mother still treats him like a baby. My new stepdad spoils him, too. I wish they'd spoil me a little once in a

20

while. At least I had Nana. I could always count on her.

"Hi, I'm home," I yelled as I opened the front door.

"Up here, honey," came a distant voice.

I peeled off my wet jacket and followed the voice up the stairs to my bedroom.

"Give me a hand in here, Emily," my mom called.

I stood in the doorway and nearly gasped because, for some reason, my furniture had been moved. My bed used to be in the center of the room. Now it was against one wall.

"What's going on?" I asked.

Mom looked up with a wide smile on her face. "A big surprise," she said.

My heart leaped. Maybe I was going to get new furniture for Christmas and she was taking measurements. I'd been wanting new furniture for the longest time. Recently I'd been dropping hints about how pretty Kaitlin's bedroom was and how her furniture all matched and how grown up and modern Lexie's bedroom was. Maybe the hints were finally paying off and they were taking out the yucky hand-me-downs I'd had all my life. I wondered what the new bedroom set would be like. Would I get to choose? If so, what would I choose—pretty and feminine like Kaitlin's, or bold and exciting like Lexie's? Tough decision.

I looked from the tall brown chest to the four-poster bed and the old rag rug on the floor and I tried to picture the room of my dreams. A big grin spread across my face. "A surprise? Can you give me a hint?"

"I'm not sure that I should," Mom said. "I'm going to need some help to get everything ready in time, though. So I'd better let you in on the secret."

I was confused now. I couldn't think why she needed to get my room ready in a hurry if the surprise was going to be my Christmas present. "Why the big rush?" I asked.

"Because she gets here tomorrow," my mother said.

"Who gets here?"

"Samantha," my mother said. "Samantha is coming tomorrow."

I just stood there with my mouth open. "That's the big surprise?" I said in disbelief. "That Samantha is coming tomorrow?"

My mother was still smiling as if she was excited. "Her mother called today and said she's got to fly to New York for an unexpected business trip. She wondered if Samantha could come to us earlier than planned, and of course we said yes. So now she'll be with us for a whole month. Isn't that wonderful?"

"Oh, sure," I muttered. "Just fabulous."

The smile faded from Mom's face. "You don't sound too thrilled."

"I don't like Samantha at all. She's a stuck-up snob."

My mother laughed nervously. "But you guys seemed to be getting along so well at the wedding. Every time I looked at you, you were busy talking."

"She was busy telling me how fat and ugly I am," I said.

Mom laughed again, more nervously this time. "Oh, Emily, that's not true. I'm sure she didn't say that."

"She did. Maybe not in those exact words."

"You can't be so self-conscious. Just because Samantha is very . . . developed for her age, you don't have to feel inferior. Everybody grows at a different rate. I'll bet you're about to blossom into a lovely young woman."

"Thanks," I said.

"Maybe Samantha will have some tips for you on clothes and hairstyles. She always dresses so nicely."

"Great, Mom," I said. "She's already told me that the dress I wore to the wedding was repulsive and made me look like a tub of flowers."

"Emily! I'm sure she didn't. You looked just adorable in that dress."

"Samantha didn't think so. She thought it made me look like a five-year-old. In fact, she spent the whole time bragging to everyone how much more grown up she was than I am."

Just then a terrible thought hit me. "Why are you moving furniture around in my room?" I asked. "She's not sleeping in here, is she?"

Mom smiled nervously again and cleared her throat. "Ed thought it would be a great way for you two to get to know each other and for Samantha to feel part of the family."

"She's not part of the family and I don't want to get to know her better! Why can't she have the guest room?"

"Emily, why are you being difficult?" Mom said.

"The guest room is way at the back of the house. We don't want her to feel cut off, do we?"

I didn't answer that, but she got my message from the way I stood glaring at her.

"Samantha is Ed's daughter and he misses her," my mom said firmly. "It's only right that we should try and make her feel welcome here."

Mom came over to me and put her arm around my shoulders. "These things always take time, Emmy. It's never easy to adjust to a new relationship, but we all have to work at it, don't we?"

I shrugged her arm off my shoulders and walked over to my dresser. "I was trying to be nice before. She was the one being insulting."

"I'm sure she didn't mean it," Mom said. "You can't judge what a person is really like from the way they behave at a wedding. When Ed took me down to meet her last year I thought she was a sweet little thing."

My back was to her, so I made silent gagging noises and rolled my eyes. There was no way I'd describe Samantha as a sweet little thing. A piranha, maybe, or a vampire, but definitely not sweet or little.

Mom must have sensed what I was doing, or at least how I felt. "And I expect you to work very hard at this, too, Emily," she said. "She's part of our extended family now, whether you like it or not."

"Not," I whispered loud enough for just me to hear.

"Okay, so let's get working," Mom said brightly. "I'll clear out two of these drawers and you make half the closet clear for Samantha's things."

"Half my closet? Mom, that's not fair. I don't have enough room as it is."

"And you're always the one who tells me you have no clothes." Mom laughed. She always seemed to have an answer for everything.

"Can't Samantha put her clothes in the guest room?"

"She can hardly walk all the way to the back of the house every time she wants to change clothes, Emmy. Be reasonable."

"I don't think taking away half my closet space is reasonable," I snapped. "I think it's very unfair. If Ed wants her to stay so much, then let her put her clothes in *his* closet!"

"That's enough, Emily," Mom said in a voice that warned me I'd better cool it. "I've made the space for Ed to bring in another bed tonight and I'll leave you to go through your closet and decide what can go into boxes for now."

"Fine," I muttered. "I'll just go to school in one pair of jeans for the next three weeks." I stomped across the room to the closet and then I let out a big yell. My precious horse collection, which always stood on the wide window ledge, was now in a big box on my bed. "Why did you take down my horse collection?"

"I thought Samantha might want to display a few things of her own, like photos and stuffed animals, just in case she's homesick."

I hope she is homesick, I thought. If she's homesick enough, then maybe she won't stay and I can get my room back.

My little brother, Robbie, appeared in my

doorway. "What happened? I heard you yelling."

"She took down my horse collection so that Samantha can put up her dumb photos," I grumbled. "I can't go to sleep unless I look at my horses."

"You're lucky," Robbie said. "You get to have Samantha sleep in your room. Now you won't be scared if you wake up in the dark."

I gave Robbie a hug. "You can have her sleep in your room if you want," I whispered.

"Of course Samantha wouldn't want to share Robbie's room," Mom said. "It's too small anyway."

"And you couldn't put his bug collection away in a box in the attic," I said. "The bugs would all die."

"I'm going to show her my bug collection," Robbie said proudly. "I'll bet she'll like my ant farm, right, Emmy?"

I couldn't exactly see Samantha going wild with joy over a bunch of ants, but I didn't want to make Robbie feel bad, so I just nodded.

"Mom says we're getting a new sister," Robbie went on. "Now I've got two big sisters to baby-sit me, right, Emmy?"

"Robbie, why don't you go paint Samantha one of your nice pictures," Mom said wisely before I strangled him.

"Okay," Robbie said happily. "Should I make a picture of my ants or the horses?"

"Whatever you do best," Mom said.

"Ants. I just have to do black dots."

"And I'll put this stuff up in the attic, Emily,"

26

Mom said, sweeping up an armful of my possessions, "while you finish off your closet."

She went, leaving me alone in the wreckage of my room. It was all so unfair, I decided as I stared at my closet. I was the one person who didn't want Samantha to come and I was the one who was going to be stuck with her twenty-four hours a day.

I walked over and sank down on my bed. I thought about my mom's excited face and Robbie rushing off to paint Samantha a picture, and I felt scared and empty inside. What if she came and they liked her better than me? What if she became the big sister in the family and nobody even noticed I was around anymore? It had been hard enough for me getting used to the idea of Ed in the house. To tell you the truth, I still hadn't gotten used to it. I hated it when he put his arm around my mother. I hated it even more when he tried to act all affectionate to Robbie and me. He isn't my father and he never will be!

All through dinner my mom and Ed and Robbie talked nonstop about Samantha. Ed told them how she had won trophies and hundreds of blue ribbons for swimming and how she learned to swim when she was only three. Robbie was very impressed because he was learning to swim right now.

"So—I won blue ribbons for horseback riding, didn't I, Mom?" I said loudly.

"Of course you did," my mom said. "Maybe Samantha would like to go horseback riding while she's here."

I remembered Lexie's idea. I'd definitely go

horseback riding with Samantha if we could find her a wild and mean horse. Then we'd watch it run away—with her on it.

"Sure," I said, grinning at the thought. "Good idea, Mom. It's been ages since I went for a good canter."

"Sounds great to me," Ed said. "We'll have to make a list of all the fun things to do around here so that we can keep Sammy entertained for the vacation. You ladies can take her shopping in San Francisco and maybe to *The Nutcracker*. . . ."

"*The Nutcracker?*" I asked. Every year I'd asked to see *The Nutcracker* and now that Samantha was coming, we were going to go, just like that. Of course with Samantha there, it probably wouldn't be too much fun anyway.

"And I can take her out looking for ladybugs," Robbie said seriously.

Mom and Ed laughed as if this was cute. I couldn't even manage a smile. I was thinking about my Christmas vacation, ruined by having to play lady-in-waiting to Queen Samantha.

After dinner I cleared the table while Ed put everything in the dishwasher. Mom went to check on a couple of mares who were going to foal soon. Robbie folded the napkins and put the place mats away in the dining room.

I was alone in the kitchen with Ed.

"I really want you and Samantha to be good friends," he said in the hearty voice he used when he was trying to be sincere. "She's been through a hard time recently. She's never really gotten over the divorce."

I stared at him coldly. "What about me?" I demanded. "You don't think it was tough on me? I love my dad and he travels so much now I never get to see him." I didn't add that I was stuck with Ed instead, but he got the message.

"I know it's been tough for you, too, Emily," he said. "Divorce is never easy on anyone, but at least your mom and I are trying to make this into a happy family for you. Samantha's mother is at work late almost every night. It's lonely for Samantha being home alone so much."

I didn't say anything, but I put the dishes down noisily beside the sink.

"My ex-wife—Samantha's mother—is very much into her new job. She doesn't really give Samantha the attention she needs. That's why I want to make sure we all have a very merry Christmas together."

I started to walk back to the dining room. "I'll go get the casserole," I said.

"Emily," he called after me. I turned back. "What?"

"I get the feeling you're not too happy about this," Ed said.

"Nobody asked me if I wanted Samantha to share my room," I said. "I don't think it's fair."

"It was my idea," he said. "I wanted my two daughters to get to know each other better."

"I'm not your daughter," I said. "I already have a father and he moved away."

"Then I'd like us at least to be friends," he said.

"You're not even making an effort, Emily. Young Robbie doesn't seem to have a problem accepting me."

"Maybe he's too young to remember what it was like with his real father," I said.

"From what I hear from your mother, life wasn't a bed of roses when your real father was around," Ed said.

"Don't you say anything bad about my father," I shouted. "He was great. He was fun and he made me laugh and taught me to ride and I miss him. So don't ask me to pretend that everything's okay, because it's not."

This time I ran out of the room.

"Emily, come back here right now," Ed yelled.

But I didn't stop. "You can't tell me what to do. You're not my father," I yelled after him as I raced up the stairs.

I was crying by the time I got to my room. I wanted to fling myself down on my bed and wrap myself in the quilt that my other grandma, Grandma Delgado, had made for me, but there was still a big box of stuff on my bed and no horses to look down at me from my windowsill.

I thought about running over to Nana's cottage, but the rain had now turned into a downpour. So I just stood there at the window, watching the raindrops run down it until I wasn't sobbing anymore.

I took the stupid box from my bed and put it out in the hallway. Then I shut my door and curled up into a little ball under the quilt. I heard my mom putting Robbie to bed and calling out to him, "Night-night, sleep tight, don't let the bedbugs bite," and I felt the tears stinging at my eyes again.

Then, instead of going downstairs, I heard her footsteps stop outside my door. She tapped lightly, then came in.

"Are you asleep, honeybun?" she whispered. I didn't answer but she came across to my bed anyway. She sat down beside me and hugged me and then tucked me in, just like she did when I was Robbie's age. She told me she knew how rough it was and how we hadn't even been a new family for a year yet. It was going to take a while to get used to it, she said, but she wanted me to try really hard for her sake. I just nodded and snuggled into my quilt. I felt really, really alone.

FOUR

The next morning I couldn't wait to see Kaitlin. I'd felt too upset to call her the night before. Besides, I'm only allowed to use the phone in the kitchen. I can't use the one in Mom's bedroom or her business line in the office, and I didn't want her and Ed listening in.

The bus seemed to take forever going from my house to Kaitlin's stop. Pee Wee was in the seat behind me and he was being his usual horrible self.

"Hey, Delgado, are you getting a zit?" he asked, jabbing me in the back with his big fat finger. "Your face is all blotchy."

"Quit poking me or I'll tell the driver," I snapped. I knew my face was blotchy. It always is after I've been crying. I'd spent hours splashing cold water all over it, but it hadn't helped. My eyes were red, too. I wasn't wearing my glasses because they make my eyes look so big and I didn't want everyone to notice them.

Kaitlin noticed right away, of course. "Emily, what's wrong?" she whispered as she got onto the bus behind her brother and sank into the seat beside me. "Are you sick? You don't look good."

A wonderful thought struck me. Maybe I was sick. Maybe I had something catching like the measles or scarlet fever and I'd have to be shut up alone for the entire holiday season. Perhaps I could go to the school nurse and convince her that I was really ill. Then she'd send me home with a note and everyone at home would be sorry they'd been so mean to me. . . .

"It could be the measles," I said.

Kaitlin laughed. "It's not the measles. Measles gives you a lot of little red spots."

"Then maybe I have something else that's very contagious."

"Do you want to be contagious?"

I nodded. "I want to be shut away for the next month."

Kaitlin laughed nervously. "Why? Think of all the things you'd miss—our skit and the holiday party and caroling and Christmas presents."

"And Samantha," I added. "She's not just coming for vacation now. She's arriving today. Ed's going to pick her up at the airport this afternoon. And my mom and grandma are already baking every kind of cake and bread in the world."

"Wow," Kaitlin said. "What a shock. When did you find this out?"

"After school yesterday," I said. "It took me by surprise. Her mom has to go to New York, so they all thought it would be a great idea if she came earlier. Everyone else is so excited about it, but they're not the ones who have to share a room with her."

"She's sharing your room?"

33

I made a face. "It was Ed's idea. He thought we'd get to know each other better."

"It might be a good idea, Emily," Kaitlin said cautiously. "You could at least try to like her."

"A good idea?" I nearly shouted the words. "Are you serious?"

"Sorry," she said. "I didn't mean . . ."

"And I didn't mean to yell," I said quickly. "It's just from what I've already seen, there is nothing about her I'd like to get to know better. You don't understand what she's like, Kaitlin. She makes me feel like one of Robbie's ants—like she could squash me at any minute. I'm counting on you guys to help me out. Maybe I could come and stay with one of you if it gets too bad at home."

"You know you can always count on us, Em," Kaitlin said. "I'd ask my mom if you could come stay with us, but it wouldn't work, would it? You know it would just make your parents mad at you. They want you and Samantha to be friends, don't they?"

I shrugged. "Who knows? The way they were acting last night, I got the feeling that maybe they'd be happier if the family was just Samantha and Robbie. I don't seem to matter."

"Oh, Em, I'm sure that's not true," Kaitlin said. "Anyway, you matter to me and Lexie."

I looked out the window because I thought I might start crying again and then my face would be even more blotchy and disgusting.

Lexie and Kaitlin were extra nice to me all day, but I could tell they didn't really understand. They

34

thought I was making a big deal about nothing. And they still believed, I could tell, that getting a new sister my own age was really a good thing. Just wait till they met her, I thought angrily. Then they'd see for themselves.

I walked very slowly down the road to our house that afternoon. I knew that Samantha would be waiting inside and I'd have to try and be nice to her. At least this time she'd be around long enough so that the rest of my family got a chance to see her meanness in action. Maybe they wouldn't think she was so wonderful when they saw what she was really like.

I pushed open the door cautiously. There were voices coming from the kitchen.

Robbie came rushing out, his face all bright and excited. "Guess who's here, Emily!"

"I have no idea—a Mighty Morphin Power Ranger?"

"No, silly," he said, giggling at my dumbness. "It's Samantha. She came. I'm going to show her my bug collection."

"Where are you, Emily? Come and meet Samantha," my mother called in the sort of phony, breathless voice she used when she was talking to strangers on the phone.

I took a deep breath and went into the kitchen. Samantha was sitting at the table with Ed on one side and my mother on the other. She looked even more grown up than I remembered her, in tight black jeans and a huge black sweater. Something was different about her. Her long blond hair, which she'd worn up for the wedding, was now cut very short and fashionable, like you see on magazine covers. And she was wearing makeup.

"They got here just before you did," Mom went on before I could say anything. "The plane was delayed. Bad weather in L.A."

"There was this incredible thunderstorm," Samantha said in a bored-sounding voice. "And when we finally took off it was so bumpy they couldn't even serve drinks."

"You must have been scared," Mom said.

"Oh, no. I'm used to flying. I take planes all the time," Samantha said. "I've been on way worse flights than that one."

"You must be starving," Mom said hurriedly. "And you too, Emily. Sit down, sweetie pie. Now, Samantha, what will you have? This one's banana bread and these are oatmeal muffins and this is our special apple cake."

"Oh, no thank you," Samantha said.

"They're very good. Especially the apple cake," Mom insisted. "Emily just loves the apple cake—don't you, darling?"

"I'm sure she does, but I'm trying to watch my weight," Samantha said. How was that for a put-down? I glanced at my mother to see if she'd noticed, but she was calmly cutting me a large slice of cake.

"Watch your weight? You're only twelve years old," Ed exclaimed. "Really, Samantha, what foolish ideas has your mother been putting into your head?

You're a growing girl. You can eat what you want."

"For your information, Daddy, girls are almost full grown at twelve," Samantha said, "and it's good to start healthy eating habits early." She looked at me critically. "I could give you some diet tips if you like, Emily."

"Emmy's not fat," my mother exclaimed. "I was kind of chubby at the same age, but then I grew up and all the extra pounds vanished. With the amount of work we do around the ranch, it's hard not to burn off what we eat."

"Speaking of ranch work," Ed said, getting up from his seat. "Why don't I do Emily's chores so that she can take Samantha upstairs and help her get settled in?"

"Good idea, darling," my mother said, getting up and giving him a peck on the cheek.

"You have to do chores, like on a real farm?" Samantha said, wrinkling her little button of a nose.

"Of course. This is a real farm," Ed said. "You never get a day off when you keep animals, right, hon?"

"Don't I know it," Mom said. She drained the last of her mug of tea. "And that foal is colicky again. I hope I don't have to get the vet tonight."

I got up, too. "You want to come upstairs? I'll show you my room." I emphasized the *my*.

"I've already taken up your bags, honey," Ed called after us.

"Thanks, Daddy," Samantha called back.

I made a face as I pushed open my door. "Thanks,

Daddy," I mouthed to myself. I thought she was supposed to be so grown up and she still called him Daddy!

"This is my room. Ed brought in an extra bed for you."

"You don't have a guest room?"

"Yes, we do. But they thought we'd get to know each other if we shared."

"I'm not used to sharing," Samantha said. "I don't know if I can sleep with someone else in the room."

"Well, don't look at me," I snapped. I'd had enough of being polite. "It wasn't my idea, believe me. I wasn't exactly thrilled about giving up half my closet space."

Samantha picked up the smaller of her two bags and put it down on my bed. "I'll take this bed." She walked across and opened the closet. "Is this all the closet space there is?"

I nodded.

"It's so small."

"I know. I had to take out half my stuff to make room for you."

"My things will never fit in here," she said. "How do you survive?"

"I guess I don't have much choice."

She eyed my things critically. "I guess you don't have many clothes, either. All I see are jeans and overalls. How boring."

I wanted to say that I'd like nice clothes, too, but I kept quiet. She opened her giant suitcase and started taking out one outfit after another. "Still, I suppose you don't need many clothes working on a farm."

"It's a ranch, not a farm."

"Same difference," she said. She picked up a bright red-and-black jacket. "Don't you just love this?" she asked. "It came from Carole Little."

"Is she a girl in your class?"

Samantha flung herself back onto the bed in a phony display of hysterics. "A girl in my class? That is sooo funny! Just wait until I tell Mom. Wait until I tell my friends. They'll just die."

"What's so funny?" I demanded. I could feel my cheeks glowing bright red.

"Carole Little is a famous fashion designer," she said, rolling her eyes to the ceiling.

"Well, excuse me. How was I supposed to know?" I demanded.

"I guess you wouldn't," she said, giving me that annoying smile. "I don't suppose anyone in your family ever wears designer clothes. My mom has to wear them all the time because she has a career."

"My mom has a career, too," I said.

"I meant a real career in the business world, where you have to look good every day. My mom always looks so great. I got this jacket from her. She bought it for herself and then she didn't like it so she gave it to me. I get tons of stuff that way."

I was glad when Robbie burst in to interrupt this exciting discussion. "When are you coming to see my bug collection, Samantha?" he asked, gazing at her adoringly.

"In a minute. We're still busy in here," she said.

"Okay. In a minute. I'll be waiting. I'll tell the bugs you're coming," he said, and rushed out.

"Is that child normal?" Samantha asked me.

"Sure he is," I said indignantly.

"I mean, isn't it kind of weird to collect bugs?" She was giving me another dose of her superior smile. "Or are you too far from town to collect pogs or stamps or other stuff that normal kids collect?"

"Robbie just happens to like bugs," I said. "He always has."

"Like I said. Weird kid." Samantha returned to hanging her clothes in my closet, pushing my stuff farther and farther into the corner to make room for her zillions of outfits.

"Maybe I'll leave some of these for you when I go home," she said. "I'll bet you'd love to wear something other than these old jeans." She picked up one of my pairs of overalls, then let them fall again. "And maybe I can help you fix your hair so that it doesn't look so blah. And I can show you how to put on makeup properly . . ."

"Thanks, but I'm not allowed to wear it yet," I said.

She gave a phony laugh. "Silly me. I keep forgetting you're so much younger than me."

"Only six months."

"Everyone grows up so much quicker down in L.A."

"I'm not in any hurry to grow up, thanks," I said. "I kind of enjoy being eleven."

She sighed and crammed yet another long flowery

40

dress into my closet. "I don't really know why I brought all this stuff," she commented. "I'm out here in the boonies. I don't suppose your animals will care if I wear designer clothes or not."

"No, I don't suppose they will," I said calmly.

She spun around and frowned at me. That wasn't the answer she wanted.

"Do you guys ever get into town and do fun stuff?" she asked. "I'll die of boredom if I'm stuck out here. At home my mother and I always go to movies and the theater."

"My mom's planning to take us to the ballet in San Francisco," I said, pleased that I had come up with something pretty special.

"Not *The Nutcracker* again? Oh, please! I have seen that so many times and it is so juvenile."

"Fine, you can stay home if you don't want to come," I said. "It will be great to have someone to do our afternoon chores for us so we don't have to rush back."

She frowned again. She obviously wasn't expecting meek little Emily to think of any brilliant comebacks. I grinned to myself. Maybe having a brain would be useful after all.

FIVE

When we came downstairs we saw that my grandmother had come over and was sitting on the big sofa by the fire.

"Hi, Nana," I called, and I ran over to give her a big hug. At last I had an ally in the room. Nana hugged me back and smiled at me.

"I asked Nana to come over to meet Samantha," Mom said.

"Little Samantha," Nana said. "Let me take a look at you. My, aren't you a grown-up young lady? How old are you, thirteen?"

"Almost," Samantha lied.

Nana patted the sofa beside her. "Come sit here so that we can get to know each other better."

Samantha sat immediately. "Can I call you Nana?" she cooed sweetly. "I've always wanted a grandmother. I don't even remember my own grandparents."

"Of course you can call me Nana," Nana said, looking pleased. "I'm going to love having another grandchild to spoil." She took Samantha's hand. "You mustn't forget to write down all the things you want Santa Claus to bring you."

"Santa Claus? I'm a little too old to believe in Santa Claus," Samantha said.

"Samantha, shhh," I said, nodding across to Robbie.

"Don't tell me he still believes? He's way too old. I found out when I was three," she said.

"Found out what?" Robbie asked, looking from one face to the next.

"Nothing, honey. Dinner's almost ready," Mom said. "Maybe you girls can help me carry in the food."

"Why don't we let Samantha take it easy tonight?" Nana said. "She's had a long trip and we're just starting our little chat. Emily can handle it, can't you, dear?"

Oh, sure. Good old Emily, I thought as I stomped through to the kitchen. Just call me Cinderella. I'm surprised they didn't kick me out of my bedroom and make me sleep on straw in the stables. I could understand my mother trying to be nice to Samantha, but my own grandmother—someone who wasn't related to her in any way! She didn't have to be so nice to Samantha, did she? Not when she already had a granddaughter of her own to love and take care of.

As I walked into the kitchen I heard Nana say, "Ask Emily to show you where I live and then you can come visit me."

"I'll come every day," I heard Samantha answer.

I didn't hang around to hear any more.

After dinner Samantha didn't even help clear the table, saying she had to finish arranging her stuff.

She'd hardly gone upstairs when there was a scream, then another, louder, scream and a huge wail from Robbie.

We all rushed up the stairs.

"She killed Frederick!" Robbie yelled.

"Frederick?" Ed asked.

"My potato bug. He was my favorite. I gave him to her as a present and she stomped on him."

Mom wrapped him in her arms. "I'm sure she didn't mean to, honey."

"Yes, she did. She said, 'Yuck, get this horrid thing away from me,' and then she stomped on him."

"Of course I killed it. How was I to know?" Samantha demanded. "I come in and found a disgusting bug on my bed."

Mom led a sobbing Robbie away to his room.

Samantha glared at me. "How was I to know?" she demanded again. "Well, at least maybe that will stop him from hanging around me. The kid was getting to be a creepy little pest."

"That creepy little pest is your new brother," I said. "We were trying hard to be nice to you, because our mother asked us to, but we won't anymore. You're the biggest pain I've ever met."

Samantha picked up her toilet bag and stomped off to the bathroom. I stood there alone in my room, my heart beating very fast. I'm not usually the kind of person who says stuff like that. Usually I'll do anything to avoid a fight. But ever since Samantha came into my life, I'd acted so different. And this time Samantha had gone too far. There was no way I was going to try to be nice to her anymore.

I looked around my room, wondering if I was in the wrong place. Samantha's junk covered every surface. Where my horse collection used to be there was now a makeup case, a hairbrush, shampoos, conditioners, and heaven knows what else. There was a big photo of her mother and Ed on my chest of drawers, which I thought was pretty tacky. A boom box with zillions of tapes lay all over what used to be my bed. In the room next door I could hear Robbie still crying.

"I have to find a way to get rid of you, Samantha," I muttered to myself. I couldn't wait to get to school in the morning. Lexie would help me figure out something really terrible. It had to be so bad that it would make Samantha decide she didn't want to stay here any longer. I felt hot all over as I thought of it. Like I said, I'm usually a quiet, easygoing sort of person. I'd just never had to handle someone like Samantha before.

The next morning there was a hitch to my plans. Mom and Ed calmly announced that Samantha would be going to school with me until vacation.

"Mom, does she have to?" I wailed.

Mom glanced at the door to see if Samantha had heard. "Shhh," she said, putting her finger to her lips. "That's not nice, Emily. She'd be bored alone here all day. I thought of giving her a couple of days to settle in, but I'm really busy right now. The vet's coming

45

over this morning to see the sick foal and I've got a Christmas order of goats to ship. Anyway, it's all arranged with your principal. Ed's already enrolled her. And it will be nice for her to meet your friends."

"She won't want to know my friends," I said.

"Of course she will. She needs friends while she's here."

"I can't imagine anybody who'd want to be her friend," I muttered.

There was nothing I could do to make Mom change her mind. She packed us both a lunch, even though Samantha said that she didn't eat sandwiches, and then she drove us to school in the minivan. I don't know if she thought I might dump Samantha on the way if she let us take the bus. I had considered it but I didn't see how.

Kaitlin and Lexie were already in our homeroom when I came in.

"Emily! We thought you really did have the measles," Kaitlin called. "Did your wicked stepsister arrive?"

I nodded over my shoulder and Kaitlin blushed bright red. She blushes easily, like me. Nothing ever makes Lexie blush. She is always cool, except for the time when she thought Mr. Meany was a werewolf. She went right up to Samantha.

"Hi, I'm Lexie," she said.

Samantha's eyes traveled up and down Lexie.

"Is it seventies day?" Samantha said, eyeing Lexie's floral bell bottoms and her tie-dyed headband.

"No, why?" Lexie demanded.

"I just wondered. Do you always dress like that?"

46

Now perhaps my friends would see that I wasn't making it up when I told them how obnoxious she was.

"Lexie always wears the most interesting clothes," I said.

"Really?" Samantha couldn't have looked less convinced.

"And this is my other friend, Kaitlin," I said.

"Hi," Samantha said, as if Kaitlin were a passing worm.

At that moment a loud voice echoed across the classroom. "Cindy, you are just incredible! I don't believe it—and what did he say to you?"

Samantha spun around as Cindy Crawley and her clique swept into the room. Cindy was the sixth-grade superstar, in her own opinion at least. She acted like she owned the sixth grade. If you were in Cindy's inner circle you mattered—if you weren't you were a nobody. We weren't exactly her archenemies anymore, not since we'd helped save her from Pee Wee's egg-and-toilet-paper attack on Halloween night, but she still thought we were pretty lame—and we were definitely not part of her clique.

"He said he couldn't believe that I—" She broke off as she saw Samantha standing there.

It was one of the great meetings of history. Cindy and Samantha clearly both thought they were the most important person in the universe as they stood facing each other.

"Hi there," Cindy said. "Are you new?"

"No, just visiting," Samantha said. "I'm staying here a while with her."

She jerked her head in my direction.

"With Emily?" Cindy asked. Samantha might as well have said she was sleeping in the homeless shelter.

Samantha nodded. "My dad married her mother. Weird, huh?"

Cindy nodded in sympathy. "And you've got to come to school with her? How boring for you. You're not really a sixth grader, are you?"

I held my breath to see if she'd tell an outright lie.

Samantha nodded again. "I had to repeat a grade, because I missed so much school when we kept traveling around. We used to live all over the world, you know, when my dad worked for a major oil company."

"Wow." Even Cindy was impressed. "Like what countries?"

"Saudi Arabia," Samantha said. "We lived there for a while, then Venezuela . . ."

"Wow," Cindy said again.

I was staring, too. I had no idea that Ed had ever traveled all over the world for a major oil company. All I knew was that he worked for a winery. I thought he'd always done that. It occurred to me that I'd never really talked to him since he came to live with us. In fact, I'd gone out of my way not to talk to him.

Cindy and Samantha were smiling at each other in a mutual admiration society.

"Nice haircut."

"Shylocks on Rodeo Drive in Beverly Hills. My mom always goes there."

"Wow. And neat boots."

"Cute sweater," said Amy Rosenberg, one of Cindy's sidekicks.

I caught Lexie's eye and she did her gagging imitation.

"I'm Cindy, by the way."

"Samantha."

"Nice name. There's an extra seat next to Amy, Samantha," Cindy said, "and we always eat lunch on the top of the bleachers when it's raining. Ask Emily to show you where. You're very welcome to join us."

"Thanks," Samantha said. She picked up her backpack and was just heading to the seat Cindy had shown her when Pee Wee, Darren, Tommy, and all the disgusting boys came in.

Pee Wee looked at Samantha's short blond hair, the hint of makeup, the high black boots, the leggings and miniskirt, and he gave a loud wolf whistle.

I hadn't even realized that Pee Wee knew what girls were before, except as people to tease.

"You new here?" he asked.

Samantha looked at Pee Wee as if he were a large cockroach. "No, I've been here since September. You just didn't notice," she said smoothly. Cindy and her friends giggled.

I could see Pee Wee's brain figuring out if this could be true.

"Didn't I see you on MTV?" he said, turning back to grin at his friends.

"I thought I saw *you* on MTV," Samantha shot back. "On *Beavis and Butt-head.* I know which one you were."

Cindy's group laughed out loud this time. "Good one, Samantha," someone called.

Pee Wee scowled. He knew he was being insulted but he hadn't quite figured out how yet.

"What's she doing here?" he asked Ryan Sanders, a boy in the class.

"She's staying with Emily Delgado."

"Delgado?" He turned around to glare at me. "That explains it. No wonder she's so stuck up."

Great, I thought. Now he'll start making my life miserable again. He'd been picking on me since we were in kindergarten together and I'd been assigned to help him learn the alphabet. I was class monitor and teacher's pet and I became Pee Wee's instant enemy. Not much had changed. He still loved to tease me out of habit.

Samantha came to all my classes, telling me how bored she was and how backward our school was with no computers and interactive stuff. Then we went to PE last period before lunch. I was kind of looking forward to seeing Samantha go through a Meany torture session.

While everyone put on their gym uniforms, Samantha changed into spandex shorts and an aerobics halter top.

"You're going wear that?" I asked.

"Sure, why not?"

Everyone stared at Samantha as we walked to the gym. Just as we stepped inside she grabbed my arm. "Who is that?" she whispered. It was the first time she'd spoken to me like an actual person.

"That's Mr. Meany, the PE teacher."

"What a hunk!" She sighed. "You guys are lucky."

"Wait until you see what he puts us through. He's a killer," I said. I felt myself blushing because I'd just realized I had a perfect opportunity for an actual conversation with him.

"Come on," I said to Samantha. "I'll introduce you."

We walked up to Mr. Meany. "This is my stepsister, Samantha. She's staying with us for a while," I said.

"Hi, Samantha," Mr. Meany said. "I see you're dressed for aerobics. That's what we'll be doing today."

"Aerobics?" Samantha squealed, and danced up and down. "I just love aerobics."

"You do?" Mr. Meany had that suspicious smile on his face.

"Sure. I do aerobics with my mom every morning at home. We have a great tape. It's called *Power Babes*."

"Then you'll find this a piece of cake, just like everyone else—right, people?"

The whole class groaned. Mr. Meany turned on the music tape and we started. After ten minutes, everyone was gasping—everyone except Mr. Meany and Samantha, that is. She was still going strong, chanting loudly, "And one and two and three and four and push and push and push and push."

"Good going, Samantha. Everybody watch how Samantha lifts her knees. Excellent."

"I've got some great routines my mom taught me from her health club," Samantha said, beaming at him. "Really fun stuff. This is all too lame for me."

"Why don't you show me at the end of class?" Mr.

Meany said. "I think these guys are ready to move on to something a little more challenging."

I sidled closer to Lexie and Kaitlin. "Now do you see what I mean? Is she the world's biggest pain or what?"

Lexie glared at Samantha's bouncing legs. "Definitely a pain in the buns of steel," she said. "We have to do something about her."

SIX

"I don't think I'll survive a month of her," I said to Lexie and Kaitlin as we came out of the locker room. "I'll go crazy."

Kaitlin nodded. "You were right. She wouldn't be my first choice for a sister."

"She sure thinks a lot of herself," Lexie said. "Did you see how she was flirting with Mr. Meany? Totally sickening. And that spandex outfit? She really is something else."

"And the way she's been insulting Pee Wee all morning. I know he'll get back at us for that."

Lexie stopped in her tracks. "What about our sleepover tomorrow night? Does she have to be there?"

"Oh no," I groaned. "I'd forgotten all about that. She'll totally ruin our sleepover."

"Maybe she won't want to join in," Lexie suggested. "I'm sure she thinks we're too lame for her."

I shook my head. "But she's sharing my room. Where is she supposed to go?"

"Maybe we could have it at Kaitlin's house," Lexie

said. "Or even my house if my mother's not trying to study her new script."

"I'll ask my mother," Kaitlin said.

"Yeah, tell your parents it's all arranged at Kaitlin's house," Lexie said to me. "But since she has a very small bedroom, there's just room enough for three people, not four."

"And she wouldn't enjoy herself anyway," I added. "She already thinks we're so babyish. I'll tell her that we always play Barbies at our sleepovers and watch *The Little Mermaid* videos. Then she definitely won't want to come."

"Good thinking, Em. Let's hope your parents agree," Lexie said. "Tell them that just because she's your sister, she doesn't have to share every part of your life. I'll bet your mom doesn't go to football games with your dad."

I grinned. "Actually in our house it's my mother who's the Forty-Niners fan. My stepfather's not interested."

"There's your example," Lexie said. "I'll bet she doesn't drag him to games. You have to have your own life."

It sounded so convincing when Lexie said it. I almost thought about asking her to come home with me to convince my folks. But it was just me and Samantha who walked up the road to the house together at the end of a long, stressful school day. Not that I'd seen much of Samantha. She'd eaten lunch with Cindy and the snobs. But I had overheard her saying, "Get lost, blimp," to Pee Wee, which probably wasn't the smartest thing to do.

"Can we go visit Nana?" Samantha asked as the bus roared away.

I hated hearing her call *my* grandmother by her pet name. And I didn't want to sit there watching *my* grandmother making a big fuss over Samantha again. "I wouldn't call on her right now," I said. "She'll only offer you cakes and cookies and you'll say you don't want to get fat and she'll be offended."

Samantha shot me a sideways look and walked on, picking her way daintily through the puddles and muddy patches. "I'll go by myself later," she said. "She especially invited me, anyway."

I glared at her back as we walked on. Why did everything she said have to be a put-down? As we came down the road, we passed the first of the paddocks where Mom kept the miniature horses. When they heard me coming, they trotted over from their hay bin where they had been eating, all ready to be petted.

Sultan, the two-foot-high stallion, was my special favorite. He looked like a war horse that had been magically shrunk to toy size. He had a beautiful, arched neck, and he moved so gracefully as he trotted over. He pushed his head between the fence boards for me to stroke his nose. I squatted down and he snuffled at my hand, hoping I had brought him a treat.

Ever since Lexie and Kaitlin had started coming to visit, he had been totally spoiled. They were always coming over and bringing him carrots and sugar cubes. Now he expected a treat every time he saw me.

I noticed that Samantha didn't exactly coo with

delight when she saw Sultan. She certainly didn't go crazy about him the way my friends did. I glanced up at her. She was standing back from the fence with her hands on her hips, as if she was bored.

"Isn't he sweet?" I asked. "He used to come inside the house when he was a colt. And he used to pull Robbie in a miniature cart at county fairs."

Samantha shrugged. "But what exactly are they for? These horses don't have any real use, do they?"

"They look pretty," I said indignantly. "They make good pets and they need less land for breeding than larger horses."

I stood up and started to walk along the path again. Samantha caught up with me. "Why does your mother go to all that trouble raising horses you can't even ride?" she asked.

"She likes it. And they make good money, too," I said. "The foals sell for over a thousand dollars."

"My mother's a marketing director," Samantha said. "She makes megabucks."

That kind of ended that conversation. I didn't even bother to point out our pygmy goats to her. Knowing Samantha, she'd probably have suggested we use them for a barbecue Saturday night.

Soon after we got home, Samantha announced that she was going alone to visit Nana. Mom said what a good idea. I just glared.

"Mom," I said as I heard the front door close. "I've got a favor to ask. It's about the sleepover tomorrow night. Can it be at Kaitlin's house instead of here? She's sure her mom will say it's okay."

"What's wrong with here?" Mom asked.

"If it's here, then we have to include Samantha and I know she'll spoil everything. She'll tell us how baby-ish we are and make fun of everything we do."

"I'm sure she won't do anything like that," Mom said.

"You haven't seen her in action. She puts down every single thing I do."

Mom smiled uneasily. "Samantha's just feeling out of place and scared right now. People often act in a silly way when they're uncomfortable. Give her time and she'll settle in. She's really a sweet girl, you know. You two could become great friends."

"Over my dead body," I muttered.

Mom laughed and came over to wrap me in a big hug. "You are being stubborn," she said. "She's only here for a little while and I just ask you to tolerate her. What could be hard about that?"

"Everything," I said. "Right now she's over with Nana, trying to get Nana to like *her* better."

"What nonsense, Emily. Nana's just trying to make her feel welcome." She looked at me critically. "I do believe you're jealous of Samantha."

"No, I'm not. I just don't like to be around mean people. So can we go over to Kaitlin's tomorrow night, please?" I remembered Lexie's magic words that always seemed to work for her. "Pretty please with sugar on top?"

Mom laughed. "You're terrible, Emily. I'm afraid the answer's no. Ed would definitely want you to include Samantha in a sleepover and I'd like to have you here because we have a Lion's Club function to attend. I need you to keep an eye on Robbie."

"But Nana's just down the road . . ."

"I know that, but I'd rather you girls were all here. I hate always imposing on Nana. You know she likes to go to bed early these days and we won't be home until ten thirty or eleven. So I'm afraid you'll just have to make the best of it, honeybun."

"Great," I said. "It will be a really fun sleepover. A total blast. A thrill a minute. A thousand laughs. My friends will have such a bad time they'll never want to come here again."

"Emily, you sure know how to exaggerate," Mom said, ruffling my hair. I shook her away. I was mad at her and I wanted to make sure she knew it.

I was angry about the sleepover all night. How could Lexie and Kaitlin and I possibly have the fun we usually had when Miss Snobby was there to spoil things for us? I got a taste of how bad it could be when we got ready for bed that night.

"You don't even wear a bra yet!" Samantha said, looking down her nose as I peeled off my T-shirt. "I've been wearing one for a year now. I guess I'm grown up for my age in every way."

"I guess I'm just a late bloomer, like my mother says," I said. I got into bed and pulled my quilt up over my head.

The next morning I grabbed Lexie and Kaitlin the moment Samantha and Cindy greeted each other like long-lost friends.

"It's no use," I whispered. "My mom insists that we have the sleepover at my place *and* she insists we include Samantha. It's going to be the worst sleepover ever."

"I don't know," Lexie said thoughtfully. "I've been thinking about this. It could be a lot of fun. . . ."

"You've got to be kidding. How?"

Lexie looked at me with a wicked smile on her face. "You want to get rid of Samantha, right?"

"Sure, but—"

"If she really hated it here . . . I mean really, really hated it, she'd want to go home, wouldn't she?"

"I guess."

"So we make sure she really, really hates it," Lexie said. "We'll make a surefire plan."

"That doesn't seem too nice," Kaitlin said.

Lexie rolled her eyes. "You think she's nice to us? Look at the way she talks to Emily. Look at the way she's always bragging. And if we have to put up with her much longer, we'll all be doing aerobics until we drop."

"So what are you saying, Lexie?" I asked cautiously.

Lexie glanced over at Samantha, who was now in the middle of Cindy's tight little clique. "I'm saying that between now and tonight we should come up with ways to make her want to go home."

"So what will we do?" I asked.

Lexie shrugged. "You know her better than I do. What does she hate most in the world?"

"Me!" I said with a laugh. Then I shook my head.

"It's no use. I really don't know her at all. I don't know what she hates or what she's scared of."

"Then it will have to be trial and error," Lexie said grandly. "If we keep working at it all night, one thing will have to work and by morning she'll be begging to go home to L.A."

SEVEN

I didn't feel totally comfortable about Lexie's plan. Sure, I wanted to get rid of Samantha with all my heart, but I couldn't help worrying about it, too. My mother always tells me I'm a worrywart and I guess that's true. I was beginning to see that there could be problems if Samantha begged to go home. For one thing, I knew her mother had gone on a business trip to New York. So Samantha couldn't fly home to an empty house. For another thing, Ed would be mad at me if Samantha told him I'd been mean to her. And then Mom would be mad at me—and even Nana. I bet they'd all take Samantha's side. If I made Samantha want to go home early, I'd have to think of a way that made it look as if it wasn't my fault. But it wasn't going to be easy.

My head was a jumble of flying thoughts all morning as I tried to concentrate on my classes. I got called up to the board to do a math problem and the figures danced in front of me. For once, I didn't have a clue what to do with them.

"She doesn't seem so smart to me," I heard

Samantha whisper loudly. "Maybe it's easier to get into gifted programs here than it is down in L.A."

In PE she had to show us a "really fun" routine that she'd learned, which of course was way too hard for us.

"Yo, baby, look at those moves!" Pee Wee shouted. It actually made Samantha blush. It was the first time I'd ever liked something he'd done.

"If your sister stays here long enough, one day you might be as fit as she is, Emily," Mr. Meany said when I had to stop, gasping for air.

I was about to say that she wasn't my sister, but Samantha said it first. "She's not my real sister, you know. My father married her mother, so we're not really related." She turned to Cindy and the snobs. "Luckily there is no family resemblance," she said, loudly enough for the people around her to hear. "No one in *my* family is overweight."

"That's not a very kind thing to say about your sister, Samantha," Mr. Meany said. I was going to pretend that I hadn't heard, but I looked up at Mr. Meany in wonder. He had actually taken my side against her! I always knew he was a wonderful person.

I didn't even feel my feet touching the floor anymore as I joined in the exercises again. I decided that I'd go along with Lexie's idea after all. Samantha deserved everything that was coming to her!

I began to think up ways to scare Samantha as I went through the rest of PE class. *One two three four, bucket of water over the door. Five six seven eight, something yucky on her plate.* I wondered if I should put Lexie's pet snake, Norman, in Samantha's bed.

When class ended I had quite a few ideas. We all made for the gym door. Pee Wee Pugh got there at the same time as Samantha. "I always wanted to know what an earthquake felt like," Samantha said to him. "Now I know."

"What are you talking about?" he demanded.

"The way the floor shook every time you jumped up and down," she said, smiling at Cindy. "It was better than a ride at Disneyland."

"You'd better watch it," Pee Wee growled. "You're going to be sorry."

I grabbed Samantha's arm. "Stop annoying him. You don't know what he's like. There's all kinds of mean stuff he could do if he wanted. Besides, he lives close to us, so he could get back at us at school or at home. He could ride his bike over anytime."

"He wouldn't dare," Samantha said, glancing back in his direction.

"That shows how much you know," I said, but she'd already pushed ahead of me into the locker room. I was sure Pee Wee would dare. In fact, I kind of hoped he would do something mean. I just hoped it would involve only Samantha, and no one else in my family.

Luckily Samantha went to eat lunch with Cindy again, giving Lexie, Kaitlin, and me time to discuss our ideas.

"Okay, what did your great brain come up with, Em?" Lexie asked.

"We could put your snake into her bed," I began.

"Norman?" Lexie shrieked. "Do you realize how

scared he'd be? What if she sat on him? That really isn't fair to him, you know. He's a very sensitive boa constrictor."

"Too bad he's not a rattlesnake," I said. "One quick bite and . . . ahhhh."

"Something in the bed isn't a bad idea," Lexie said thoughtfully. "Some of Robbie's bugs, maybe?"

"He wouldn't let her squish any more of his bugs. He's still mad at her for killing his favorite one."

"How about something slimy," Kaitlin suggested, "like a frog or a lizard?"

"Most things hibernate in the colder months," I said. "I'll have to ask Robbie. He knows about bugs and things."

"We have to think this through carefully," Kaitlin said. "A frog in her bed wouldn't make her want to go home. She'd just be annoyed and tell on you. Then you'd get in trouble and you wouldn't be allowed to have any more sleepovers."

"She's right, Em," Lexie said to me. "We have to be clever and subtle. We have to scare her, but not so much that she realizes we're doing the scaring."

"Like what, for example?" I asked.

Lexie shrugged and thought for a moment. "How about ghosts? Would she be scared if she knew your house was haunted?"

"But my house isn't haunted."

"It is now," Lexie said, grinning. "How about if we hold a séance? I'm great at that kind of stuff. I used to act out ghost stories when I lived down in L.A. We'll hold a séance and make it seem like the place is haunted."

"And the ghost doesn't like Samantha being there?" Kaitlin suggested.

"Yeah." Lexie grinned. "The ghost definitely picks on Samantha. I'll see what kind of spooky stuff we've got at home. Green slime would be good, if I could make it drop from the ceiling at just the right moment. Especially on her head!"

"Lexie!" Kaitlin and I looked at each other and laughed. Lexie really does get the most outrageous ideas.

I felt excited and hopeful as we walked home that day. I was going to show that snobby Samantha that her little stepsister wasn't a person she could push around. For once I was going to get even.

At about seven that evening, my friends arrived and dumped their sleeping bags in my room. "I've found some great props for the séance," Lexie whispered, "although I couldn't find any slime."

"Should I put my stuff on your bed, Em?" Kaitlin asked, starting to unpack her pajamas and robe.

"It's not my bed anymore," I said. "I'm over there, in the corner."

"It soon will be again," Kaitlin whispered as she passed me. I grinned to myself. I was looking forward to this.

"You're sure you'll be all right?" Mom asked, fussing around as she and Ed got ready to leave. "You've got the number where we'll be. You can call Nana if you need her, and oh, make sure Robbie doesn't watch anything too scary on TV."

"We'll be fine," I said. "We're going to have fun."

"I think I'll go over to see Nana," Samantha said.

Lexie and I glanced at each other. After all our plans, she wasn't going to be here?

"I don't want you walking around in the dark, Samantha, honey," Ed said.

"This isn't the big city. It's safe out here, isn't it?" she demanded.

"I don't think you realize just how dark it is with no streetlights," Ed said. "And anyway, I think it would be nice if you got to know Emily's friends and had a chance to enjoy a sleepover. I don't suppose you're allowed to have friends over often at home."

"We've kind of outgrown sleepovers," Samantha said in a bored voice. "They're for little kids."

I didn't know what to wish right now. Part of me wished she would spend the evening with my grandmother so that my friends and I could have fun. The other part was all geared up for scaring her away.

It was now or never, I decided. "We're going to be working on our skit for the talent show, Samantha," I said. "Maybe you can help us."

"Okay," she said. "I guess I could help out. I've been in so many plays."

"Good, it's all settled," Ed said, nodding in a satisfied way. "You girls can stay up until we get home as a special treat, but behave yourselves, understand?"

"Don't worry," I said. "We'll be just fine. We're going to have lots of fun." I didn't look at Kaitlin or Lexie in case I started smiling.

We went upstairs to my room. I peeked in on

Robbie to make sure he was okay. Ever since the bug-squishing incident he had kept away from Samantha. He had put a big sign on his door saying, Do not entur. Bugs in heer. Danjer. He wanted to make sure that the rest of his bug collection stayed safe from her.

Robbie was building a Lego model. "I'm fine," he said. "Tell Lexie she can come in to say hi, and Kaitlin, but not Meany Face."

I grinned as I went to join the rest of them in my bedroom. I was just in time to hear Samantha's bored voice saying, "You still wear pajamas with teddy bears on them?"

"My grandmother sent them for my birthday last year," Kaitlin answered, "so my mom makes me wear them."

"I think they're cute," Lexie said.

"I won't wear anything but silk nightgowns," Samantha said. "I'd hate to look like a child."

"Let's start working on the skit," I said quickly before this conversation could go any further.

"Okay, show me what you've got so far." Samantha looked bored already.

"We've only gotten as far as the idea," Lexie said. "We thought we'd do a spoof on one of those Christmas stories—you know, where the mean monster steals Christmas? We want the mean monster to be Mr. Meany—and get this, he steals Christmas because everyone is too tired to celebrate. The monster makes everyone exercise, you see—or maybe he's a wicked king. We haven't worked that out yet. And we want to include some of the other teachers, too. Like Mrs. Bliese, who's really a neatness freak, but she's too tired to clean up her house for Christmas. . . ."

Lexie was talking a mile a minute. She paused and looked at Samantha. "Is that it?" Samantha asked.

"Just about."

"So what happens?"

"We don't know yet. We're just up to the basic idea."

"Sounds dumb to me," Samantha said.

"The kids at our school will think it's funny," I said. "They know the teachers."

"Making fun of teachers is okay," Samantha said. "But doing a Christmas story about a monster—that is so juvenile. It might have been okay in fifth grade, but you're going to have eighth graders watching. They'll think it's really stupid."

I glanced at Lexie. "No, it isn't," I said. But I wasn't sure anymore. What if our idea was too young for middle school? I could imagine Kaitlin's big brother, Tom, and his eighth-grade friends making loud comments and laughing at us. "Okay, we'll scrap the idea for tonight. We can work on it some other time," I said.

"So what are we going to do now?" Lexie asked.

I shrugged and looked over at Samantha.

"Don't ask me," she said. "I told you I outgrew sleepovers years ago."

"It's a shame you didn't bring your Kayla, Princess of Power doll with you, KD," Lexie said. "Then we could have played the Princess of Power game."

"Princess of Power?" Samantha asked, wrinkling her nose. "What's that?"

"Just a game we play with our Barbies," Lexie said.

I knew Lexie was just saying all this to annoy Samantha. I could see the way her eyes were twinkling.

"Don't tell me you guys still play with Barbies," she spluttered.

"All the time," Lexie said.

"Isn't it about time you grew up?" Samantha demanded. "Maybe I'll just go downstairs and watch TV and leave you little girls to your games."

Lexie and I looked at each other. How could we scare her if she wasn't even around?

"No, don't do that," I said. "Your dad wants you to get to know my friends. What would you like to do right now?"

"I could show you guys how to put on makeup," she said. "And we could give each other manicures."

"Okay," Kaitlin said before I could say anything. "I've always wanted to wear nail polish, but Mom never lets me."

I had to agree that a manicure might be fun, but not when Samantha was giving it. It was just another way of letting her show how grown up and superior she was.

Samantha got out her huge makeup bag. "I have everything in the world in here," she said.

"Do you have any black nail polish?" Lexie asked. "I only wear black."

"I don't think so," Samantha said, not realizing that Lexie was teasing her. She opened up the

69

bag. "I've got a great mud pack and . . . ahhhhh!"

Something had jumped out of the makeup bag and onto Samantha's hand. She leaped back, screaming. "Get it off me!" she yelled. She was dancing around like crazy.

"It's okay," I said. "It's only a little frog." I scooped it up off the floor before Samantha could squish it like Robbie's bug.

She glared at us, her face bright red. "You are so immature—that was such a childish, kindergarten trick to play on me."

"Hey, wait a minute," I said. "You don't think we put the frog in there."

"Then how did it get in?" she demanded. "Don't tell me it decided to take a walk all the way from its swamp up to the bedroom and then it decided to take a nap in my makeup bag."

I realized right away, of course, that Robbie must have put it there, but I wasn't about to get him into trouble. Besides, Lexie, Kaitlin, and I had talked about frogs. If we'd known how well it was going to work, maybe we would have done it ourselves.

"This is a ranch, Samantha," I said. "Like you said, this is the boonies. There are all kinds of creatures that come inside for the winter. We just get used to them. They can't hurt you—aside from the rattlesnakes . . ."

"Rattlesnakes? What rattlesnakes?"

"The ones that hibernate in warm corners of the house."

"You're just making that up," Samantha said. "I know you put the frog there."

"And I swear I didn't," I said. "Too bad if you don't believe me."

"Why don't you get out the nail polish, Samantha?" Kaitlin said.

Samantha shook her head. "You don't need to know about makeup if you're still acting like little kids. Besides, how do I know that there aren't poisonous spiders in my nail polish kit? I'm through with makeup."

"In that case," Lexie said dramatically, "it is now time for the séance."

EIGHT

"What séance?" Samantha asked in a surprised voice.

"Lexie promised we'd hold a séance when we had a sleepover at my place," I explained.

"That's right," Lexie said. "Emily told me that they always thought the house was haunted. I told her I'm very psychic and maybe we could find out if the legend is really true."

"What legend?" Samantha asked.

"That the ghost of Doña Isabella really walks at night," I said. "This house is on the site of the original Mexican adobe, you know. My mom's family has owned this land for a hundred years. Doña Isabella was her ancestor. She was very beautiful but she was killed when bandits set the house on fire." Those creative writing classes at school were paying off! I could see that Samantha was beginning to buy our story. I almost was myself.

"Okay, let's get started," Lexie said. "We need a table and a cloth and a candle . . ."

We ran around finding the things we needed. I had no idea what Lexie planned to do. We hadn't had time to talk through the plan together, but Lexie looked like she knew what she was doing. "This is exciting!" I said, and I really meant it. My heart was already racing. I was a little scared of the séance myself, even though I knew Lexie would be faking it. After all, this really was an old house and it really was on the site of a Mexican adobe. . . .

Lexie took out a black shawl and draped it over her head. Then she lit the candle. "Please take your seats around the table," she said in a low voice.

We sat. The fringe of the tablecloth tickled my hands and made me pull them back.

"Turn off the light," Lexie said.

The candle threw a flickering glow on our faces and sent shadows dancing on the walls. It was very dark and very still.

"From now on, nobody is to move or speak," Lexie said. She raised her hands. "Oh, spirit world, we wish to talk to you. Come to us now," she said in a whisper. There was complete silence. "Oh, spirits, if you are here, give us a sign," Lexie said.

A loud thump made all of us jump.

"What was that?" Kaitlin whispered.

"They are here," Lexie said dramatically. "They have given us a sign."

"This is dumb," Samantha said, but she didn't sound very sure.

"Spirit who is with us now," Lexie went on. "If you are a man, knock once. If you are a woman, knock twice."

We held our breaths. Through the darkness we heard two faint taps. *Knock, knock.*

"Spirit, are you the ghost of Doña Isabella?" Lexie asked.

The whole table began to shake. I grabbed for the candle, but my hands were trembling so much I could hardly hold it.

"She is here," Lexie said. "Now, Doña Isabella, do you have a message for us?"

The candle began to flicker, as if it was stirred by a breeze. Suddenly I heard the most unearthly noise. It was nothing like a sound Lexie could have faked. It was more like a horrible scream in the night.

All of us leaped up from the table—even Lexie.

"What was that?" Kaitlin gasped.

"Outside," Lexie managed to get out. "It was outside the window."

We ran to the window and wrenched it open. Something white flapped and fluttered past us, close to our faces. We all screamed.

It took me a couple of seconds to realize what it was. "It's okay. Relax. It's a screech owl. They have a nest in that big oak tree."

"An owl," Lexie said. "What else could it have been?" I saw she was breathing very hard.

"Okay, panic over," Samantha said. "Let's get back to our séance."

"I . . . don't think I want to do this anymore," Kaitlin said.

My heart was still racing a mile a minute. "I don't think I want to do it either," I said.

"Me neither," Lexie agreed.

"But you can't quit just when it was getting interesting," Samantha said.

"Yes, we can," I answered quickly.

Samantha burst out laughing. "What a bunch of wimps," she said. "You get scared *sooo* easily. Don't tell me you really believe in ghosts. I've played with Ouija boards a hundred times at parties, but I don't really believe that stuff."

She went over and flipped on the light switch. "I'm hungry," she said. "I'm going to go fix myself a snack."

We stood there, still breathing hard and looking at each other in despair. All our plans were going wrong. It looked as if there was no way we were going to get rid of Samantha.

"We can't let her win," Lexie said.

"Well, I'm sorry, but there was no way I was going on with that séance," Kaitlin muttered. "It was much too scary."

I nodded. "All that tapping and the table shaking . . ."

"That was *me*," Lexie said. "I was doing all those things.

I was kicking my toe against your closet door. I made the table shake with my knees. I blew at the candle . . . but that noise really got to me."

"Me too," I said.

"If only it had scared Samantha, it would have solved all our problems," Lexie said.

"So what do we do now?" Kaitlin asked.

I shrugged. "Things like frogs just make her mad. She's not scared of ghosts."

75

"I say we take her out in the dark and dump her," Lexie said angrily. "She'd never find her way home."

Kaitlin and I giggled nervously.

"Don't laugh," Lexie said. "It really might scare her if she couldn't find her way home. You know how dark it gets out here."

"And she's not used to being in the country," I said. "You should see how she tiptoes through the mud so that she doesn't wreck her expensive shoes."

"Maybe she'll fall in the mud," Kaitlin suggested. "There's lots of mud in your fields right now. And all those ditches are really full of water . . ."

"And she could run into the fences around your horse fields," Lexie suggested.

"Definite possibilities," Kaitlin agreed. "She might not think she was so wonderful if she couldn't find her way home. Now all we have to do is think of a way to lure her outside."

"A moonlight stroll?" Lexie suggested.

"There's no moon tonight," I said. "Which makes it perfect for getting lost."

"You could say you had to inspect the horses for your mother," Kaitlin suggested.

I shook my head. "She wouldn't care. She'd make me do it alone. She doesn't even like our animals."

"I know!" Lexie shouted. "We'll have a treasure hunt. We'll make a list of things we have to find, and some of them can only be found a long way from the house. You take Samantha with you, Em, because you know your way around better than we do. You take her far from the house. Then you find some excuse and you just slip away and leave her there."

"What a great idea," I said. "And it sounds easy. But what if something really happened to her?"

"What could happen to her? There are no fierce bulls on your property or rivers she could fall into," Lexie said. "The worst thing would be that she couldn't find her way home until morning . . . and she got a little wet and muddy."

"They did forecast rain for tonight," I said. I really was being torn in two. Leaving someone in the dark was such a mean thing to do. I'd never done anything that bad in my life before. But then, I'd never met anyone like Samantha before. She really deserved it.

Just then, Samantha walked in, a carrot stick in her hand. "Don't you guys have any healthy munchies?" she asked. "Everything in there is full of fat and cholesterol."

"That's the way we like it," I said. "We work on a farm. We burn calories."

"Not enough, obviously," Samantha said.

"And what does that mean?" Lexie demanded.

"That Emily could lose a few pounds," Samantha said.

"I think Emily's just fine the way she is," Lexie said angrily.

"Me too," Kaitlin said. "I think she's pretty."

"She could be, with a total makeover," Samantha said. "New 'do, contacts instead of glasses, and a whole new wardrobe."

This discussion was helping me make up my mind.

Anyone who ran me down and tried to make me look small in front of my friends deserved to be left alone in the dark.

"Shut up, you guys," I said. "Let's play a game, okay?"

"What do you want to play?" Lexie asked innocently.

"How about if we have a treasure hunt?"

"I might have known you'd pick a babyish game," Samantha said with a bored sigh. "Oh, well. What do we do?"

"We divide into teams," Lexie explained. "Then we make a list of objects and the first team that finds them all is the winner."

"Okay." Samantha was beginning to sound interested. "I'll be on Emily's team. She must know her way around here better than you guys. Who picks the objects?"

"First we pick ten objects for you and you pick ten objects for us," Lexie said. "Could you get us paper and pencils, Emily? Then we'll start."

"Just things around the house?" Samantha asked.

"And outside, too. That makes it more fun," Lexie said. I looked down as I handed everyone some paper and a pencil. I was scared I might start giggling and give the whole thing away. Lexie and Kaitlin huddled in one corner, making their list. Samantha and I made ours. "They should all be easy things to find," I called. I wrote down *safety pin, rubber band, oak leaf, horse hair, round pebble*.

"Make them harder than that," Samantha whispered, "to make sure we win."

I hadn't realized that Samantha was so competitive. This might work out well, I decided. We finished our list.

"Listen up," Lexie said. "Now we add the lists together, so that each team has to find the same things. If neither team has finished by ten o'clock, then the team that has the most items is the winner."

Samantha nodded. "Okay, when do we start?"

"When I've finished copying out the whole list for both teams," Lexie said. She quickly scribbled our list onto her paper and their list onto our paper. Then she handed us the full list. "Okay? Ready, set, *go*!"

We examined our lists. "The household items are easy," I said to Samantha.

"Let's do the outdoor stuff first," Samantha said, grabbing my sleeve. "There might not be many oak leaves around at this time of year and we want to make sure we get to them before they do."

I couldn't believe how easily our plan was working. Samantha and I ran outside. "It's okay," I called to her, "I know where there's an oak tree that will still have some leaves." I sprinted ahead of her across the yard and headed off down a path between fields.

"Do we have to go so far?" she called after me. "Isn't there an oak tree closer to your house?"

"Yes, but all its leaves are gone," I said. "This one will be perfect. Trust me."

"Slow down!" Samantha called. "I can't see where we're going."

"Follow me," I called. "I know my way."

The path joined another, smaller path and I swung to the right. The dark twisted shape of a giant oak tree loomed ahead of us, its bare twigs reaching out like evil fingers in the darkness.

"Here we are," I whispered. "See if you can find any leaves on the ground."

I heard her scrambling around. I checked to see if I could make my escape now. I started to tiptoe away, one step, two . . .

"I've got one," Samantha yelled. "What's the next thing on the list?"

At that moment a long, drawn-out howl floated on the breeze.

"What was that?" she demanded.

I knew it was our neighbor's dog, but I wasn't going to tell Samantha that. I was very tempted to say "wolves," but I thought she might not be dumb enough to believe me. Then a brilliant idea flashed into my mind. Maybe I could make her believe it was something else, something wild and fierce . . .

"Coyotes," I said excitedly. "Don't tell me they've come down again."

"Down where?"

"They come down from the hills when they're hungry," I said. "We've had so much trouble with them."

"Do they eat people?" For the first time Samantha didn't sound so sure of herself.

Again I was tempted to say yes. I didn't actually know that much about coyotes. "They come to get our baby animals," I said.

The howl came again. This time it sounded closer.

"The baby animals?" she asked.

"Yes, the foals and the baby goats," I said. "We have to stop them. Come on."

"Are you crazy?" she called after me. "I'm not fighting off wild coyotes."

"But they'll kidnap the foals. Come on, hurry up," I yelled. Then I took off as fast as I could run. I swung over the gate into the nearest field and sprinted across it. It was so dark and spooky out there and the howls were so close that I almost had myself convinced that coyotes *were* after our foals. "We have to get there in time," I called, and put on an extra sprint.

"Emily!" I heard Samantha's voice, far off in the darkness. "Wait up. Don't go without me. I can't see a thing. Emily—where are you?"

I ducked down behind a hedge and held my breath. I couldn't believe I was actually doing this. Then I climbed the gate at the far side of the field and trotted down the path to the house.

Lexie and Kaitlin were waiting in the yard with anticipation all over their faces. "Did you lose her?" Kaitlin asked. "How did you do it?"

"We heard the neighbors' dog howling and I told her it was coyotes sneaking up on the foals," I said. "I told her we had to go save them and then I just ran. I guess she couldn't keep up in the dark."

"So you really dumped her," Lexie said with excitement in her voice.

I looked around, then listened. I couldn't even hear Samantha calling out to me anymore. It was completely quiet. "Looks like we lost her," I said.

Lexie gave me a high five. "Way to go, Em. That'll teach her."

"I hope so," I said, but my nervous feeling began to return. It sure was quiet out there. What if something had happened to her? I remembered reading once that a person could drown in four inches of water. What if she fell in a ditch, hit her head, and drowned? Could they get me for murder?

"Maybe we should go look for her," I suggested.

Lexie shook her head. "Nah," she said. "Let her get really worried first. We want her to sweat. We want her to panic. We want her to think she's stuck out there for the entire night."

"Okay," I said, but I wasn't sure. I was thinking about me as much as her. I could imagine what my mom and Ed would say if they got home and Samantha was missing. I'd be in the worst kind of trouble. I'd be grounded for life, banned from sleepovers forever . . .

Then through the darkness we heard a faint sound. "Emileee?"

The howls started again. Then there was a surprised scream, snorting, scuffling, muffled cries, and groans. Lexie, Kaitlin, and I looked at each other in horror.

"You don't think there really are coyotes out there, do you?" Kaitlin whispered.

"Not around here," I said.

82

"Then what was making that noise?" Lexie demanded. "Maybe a wild dog got onto your property. You don't have any fierce animals that sound like that."

We started running in the direction of the cries. Something terrible was happening to Samantha and it was all my fault.

NINE

We stumbled forward in the darkness. Then as we turned to head down the path we stopped dead. A creature was coming toward us—a nightmare creature. A faceless, shapeless, dark-all-over thing was lurching forward.

"They got me," the creature gasped in Samantha's voice. "The coyotes got me."

We ran up to her, grabbing her as she collapsed. The words poured out in a jumble. "I tried to follow you across that field but you went too fast for me, then I thought I saw lights in this direction and I crossed into another field and I'd almost made it across when I got stuck in the mud and then—then something hit me from behind. It must have been the coyotes. They knocked me down and there was this horrible breathing in my face. I tried to cover my face with my hands before they ate me. I've never been so scared in my life. . . ."

As she talked, I suddenly realized what happened and I started laughing. I couldn't help it.

"It's not funny!" she yelled.

"Samantha, that wasn't coyotes, it was our billy goat. He hates it when strangers come into his field."

"Billy goat? What billy goat?" she demanded.

"You know, our pygmy goats I told you about. They're in the field you just came from. The billy is very aggressive. He must have knocked you down and then breathed on you. He does that. He couldn't really have hurt you. He only comes up to your knee."

"Not hurt me?" Samantha shrieked. She was hysterical now. "Look at me—I'm covered with mud. My clothes are ruined. I'm a total mess."

"You sure are," Lexie said with delight.

Samantha glared at us, then she said, "You did this, didn't you? You've been trying to play tricks on me all evening. So now you've succeeded. I hope you're happy.

"You never wanted me here, did you?" she continued. "Well, I sure don't want to be here. In fact, I hate it here. I hate this stupid farm and the stupid animals and the stupid people and most of all I hate you, Emily Delgado. I'm calling my mother and telling her to get me out of this horrible place right now!"

She pushed past us, heading for the house.

Lexie nudged me. "We did it, Em. Our plan worked," she yelled.

We made our way back to the house. There was no sign of Samantha, except for a trail of mud leading up the stairs. We followed it.

"Do you think she's calling her mom right now?" Kaitlin asked. I noticed she sounded nervous, which was just how I felt. My insides felt as if they were twisting in knots. I had expected to be so happy when I finally got the better of Samantha, but I wasn't. As we reached the top of the stairs, we heard sounds coming from the bathroom. Over the noise of running water there was the unmistakable sound of sobbing. Kaitlin and I glanced at each other.

"I hope she's okay," Kaitlin whispered.

"Sure she is. She just got scared and muddy," Lexie said. "Serves her right. Think of all the mean things she did to you, Em."

"I know," I said, "but I still can't help feeling bad. That really was a mean trick to play on someone. I didn't expect it to work so incredibly well . . . I mean, getting lost and then falling in the mud and then meeting up with the billy goat. We couldn't have planned that, could we?"

Lexie was grinning. "I'd say our plan was a total success, myself."

"So why don't we feel better?" I asked.

Nobody needed to answer me. Shuddering sobs were still coming from the bathroom. I got out the mop and cleaned up the mud trail. When I was done, Samantha still hadn't come out. We got a plate of cookies and went back to my room. We got into our pj's. Still no Samantha.

"Do you think she's going to stay in there all night?" Kaitlin asked.

"She'll probably tell Mom and Ed everything when they come home. She'll have to, if she wants to go back home," I said.

"You can say it was all an accident. It wasn't your

fault she got lost and fell in the mud and met the billy goat," Lexie said.

"But it was," I said. "It was like all our best plans added together."

"So you think you'll get in big trouble?"

I nodded.

"It will be worth it to get rid of creepy Samantha forever, won't it?" Lexie asked.

"I guess."

"You want her out of here, don't you?" Lexie demanded.

"Sure."

"Well, then," Lexie said, as if that closed the matter. She grabbed a cookie and started eating. I joined her, but the cookie tasted like sawdust and I could hardly swallow it.

A little later we heard the sound of the bathroom door opening. Samantha came out, wrapped in a towel, looking pink and freshly scrubbed. I ran out into the hall to meet her.

"Samantha, I'm sorry about what happened," I said. "I'm sorry your clothes got wrecked."

"You're not sorry," she said, pushing past me. "You wanted it to happen."

"Okay, I admit it. I wanted you to get lost," I said as I followed her to the bedroom. "And I wanted to make you scared, too. But now I'm sorry. I've never done anything mean like this in my life."

"I know why you did it," she said coldly. "You didn't want to share your room and your family. You don't want a sister. You made that very clear. And that's fine, because I wouldn't want a mean, horrible person like you for a sister anyway."

"I'm not usually mean," I said at exactly the same moment Kaitlin said, "Emily's not mean."

"She was just paying you back for all the horrible things you did to her," Lexie added.

Samantha looked surprised. "Me? When did I do anything mean to her?"

"Try all the time, Samantha," I said. "You've been nonstop mean to me since the first moment we met."

"Like when?" she demanded.

"Like when you made fun of me at the wedding. You made me feel stupid and ugly in that dress. And ever since you got here you've been telling me I'm fat and my clothes are no good . . ."

"And at school you made friends with our enemies and you bragged all the time," Lexie added.

"What enemies?" Samantha demanded.

"Cindy Crawley. You hung out with Cindy Crawley," Kaitlin said accusingly.

"How could I know she was your enemy?" Samantha demanded.

I had to admit to myself that she had a point there. I'd never told her Cindy was my enemy. But at the time it had seemed like another thing she was doing to spite me.

While I was thinking this out, my friends were still on a roll.

"And you're always making fun of Emily and treating her like a little kid," Kaitlin went on.

"And you don't only put me down. You put down

my mother and my brother, too," I said. I knew my cheeks were very pink but I was feeling braver now. "You tell us nonstop how wonderful your mother is and how much she earns and how great everything is in L.A. and Beverly Hills."

"I do not!" Samantha said, but then her cheeks began turning pink, too. "Well, maybe just a little. . . ."

"Just a *lot*, Samantha," Lexie said. "All the time. You never say anything nice to Emily. It's always a put-down."

Samantha swallowed hard. "I don't mean to talk like that," she said quietly. "I guess I say dumb things when I'm scared. You don't know how hard it is to come to a place where you don't know anybody and you're not sure you'll fit in."

"Acting snobby all the time doesn't help much, you know," Lexie said.

Samantha looked down at her feet. "I know I act snobby and superior sometimes, but it's only to tell myself I'm in control when I feel I'm not. I can hear myself, but I can't seem to stop. Was I really that bad?"

"The worst," I said.

There was a long silence. Then Samantha gave a little sigh. "Dumb, isn't it?" she said. "I was so looking forward to this—to being part of a real family for once. And now I've blown it."

"You haven't blown it, Samantha," I said quietly.

"Really?" she asked.

We stood there, looking at each other. She was taller than me, but not much. I guess I'd grown.

"We could learn to get along," I said. "I'm willing to work at it if you are."

"No kidding?" She looked up, and I saw that she was really younger looking without all that stuff on her face—at least as young as I was.

"Sure," I said. "Only I mean work at it. No remarks about my weight or my hair or my glasses. I'm really sensitive about those things. I don't exactly like the way I look right now, but I'm hoping I'll look better soon. My mom keeps saying I'll grow up instead of out soon and I have to believe her. She's promised me contacts when I'm old enough to be responsible with them. So I'm working on everything."

"I'm sorry," Samantha said. "I really wanted to help, but I see now that it came across as a put-down. I'm just not very good at knowing what to say."

"That happens to all of us, Samantha," Kaitlin said. "Everybody feels awkward sometimes. I was just dreading my first day at a new school. I didn't know anybody. But then I met Emily and she was so nice to me, and then we met Lexie and it's been great ever since. So it's not that hard to make friends, trust me."

"To make a friend you have to be a friend, isn't that what they always tell you?" Lexie said, half joking, half serious.

Samantha nodded. "Okay, I'll give it a try."

"Then let's start over," I said. "We'll pretend tonight never happened and we'll start the sleepover right now."

"Good idea," Lexie said. "In that case, let's start with food. I'm starving."

TEN

"So what do we do now?" Lexie asked as we finished the last of the plate of gingerbread cookies. They were one of my grandmother's specialties and I noticed that for once, Samantha hadn't said no to them.

"I know," Samantha said. "Let's play Truth or Dare."

"How do you play it?" Kaitlin asked.

Samantha started to laugh. "You've never played Truth or Dare?" But then she stopped herself. "It's a lot of fun," she said in a much nicer voice. "It's great for sleepovers."

"I used to play it all the time down in L.A.," Lexie said.

Samantha looked surprised. "You used to live in L.A.?"

"We still do when my mother's working," Lexie said.

Samantha looked at me. "Her mother's a movie star," I said smoothly. For once Samantha was surprised.

"No kidding?" she said. "Wow."

"She comes up here for peace and quiet when she's not working," Lexie explained. "I like it up here a lot better. The people down in L.A. are sometimes . . . you know . . . phony."

"I know what you mean," Samantha said. "It's hard to keep up there. You have to have the latest everything."

"I never worried about stuff like that," Lexie said.

"You wouldn't have to," Samantha agreed. "You're so . . . well . . . unique, and your mom's a movie star, too."

"Tell us about Truth or Dare," I said, interrupting this mutual admiration society. It was really interesting that Samantha hadn't noticed Lexie was alive until now.

"Simple," Samantha said. "When it's your turn you have a choice, to tell the truth to a question or to accept a dare that we think up for you."

"Okay," I said cautiously. "You can start and show us."

"All right, Emily," Samantha said. "Which do you want—truth or dare?"

"Truth." A dare sounded scarier than telling the truth.

"Do you have a secret crush on anybody?" Samantha asked. "Remember, you have to tell the truth."

Why didn't I pick the dare? I felt myself blushing again. "Okay." I took a deep breath and closed my eyes. "I have a crush on Mr. Meany."

"That's not a secret." Lexie laughed. "That's totally obvious. You blush every time you're around him."

I hadn't realized how obvious it was. "Okay, let's do Samantha now," I said quickly. "Which do you want?"

"Truth," Samantha said.

"Do you ever put Kleenex in your bra?" Lexie asked. Kaitlin and I started giggling.

"No problem," Samantha said. "I never needed to. I was the first one in my class to need a bra. I wanted to hide what I had, not add to it."

I noticed Samantha was blushing. "You don't know what it's like," she went on hurriedly. "All the boys make dumb remarks and all the girls think you're showing off, but you can't help the way you look."

"Hey, this is getting too serious," Lexie said. "It's supposed to be fun. Let's give someone a dare."

"A trick phone call," Samantha said. "We used to do that. It's so much fun. Get the phone book."

"It's in my mom's room. And there's a phone in there, too." I led them down the hall and into my mother's bedroom. "Okay, Lexie, how about you go first."

"Who do I call?" Lexie asked.

"Just open at any page, close your eyes, and point to a name."

Lexie did it. "Jackson. Harry and Joan."

"They sound nice and boring." Samantha laughed. "Now call them up . . ."

"What do I say?"

"Ask them if their refrigerator is running," Samantha said.

"And then what?"

"Then you say, 'Well, you'd better go catch it.'"

We all started giggling. "Go on, do it," Samantha urged.

Lexie dialed. We heard a distant hello at the other end of the line.

"Good evening," Lexie said. "Is your refrigerator running?"

She put her hand to her mouth to stop herself from laughing. "Then you'd better go catch it," she said, and hung up. We flung ourselves back on the beds, laughing. It was so funny and so terrible at the same time.

"Let's do it again," Lexie said. "Kaitlin, you go."

Kaitlin shook her head furiously. "I couldn't. I just couldn't do it."

"You have to. We dare you—it's part of the game."

"Don't I get a choice, truth or dare?"

"We changed the rules," Lexie said. "Now it's dare or dare."

"She doesn't have to do it if she doesn't want to," I said, seeing Kaitlin's worried face. "I'll go next."

"Okay," Samantha said, grinning broadly. "We dare Emily to call Mr. Meany."

"No!" I shouted.

The others started clapping. "Good one, Sammy," Lexie said. "Okay, Em. This is your big chance."

"I couldn't. I'd rather die."

"You don't have to say who it is," Samantha said. "Quick. Find his number."

"Maybe it's unlisted," I said hopefully.

"There it is," Lexie yelled, leaning over my shoulder. "M. Meany. See, I knew his first name had to be begin with *M*. I told you he liked *M* words, like Monday Mile and monster and murder."

"How do we know it's him?" I asked. I could feel the sweat trickling down my forehead at the thought of what I had to do. "It could be another Meany."

"He's the only one in the book," Lexie said. "It has to be him."

"So what do I say?"

"Listen up," Samantha said. "What we have to do now is think of the wildest, craziest first name starting with *M*."

"How about Maximilian?" I suggested.

"Didn't we think it was Melvin?"

"Maybe. I've got it—Montgomery."

"No. I've got it. Mad Dog."

We were getting silly again.

"Mr. Mad Dog Meany?" I shrieked.

"I know," Lexie said grandly. "Maurice!"

"Hey, that's good," Samantha said. "He'd never be Maurice in a million years. Okay, Emily, this is what you have to do. You dial his number. When he answers you say, 'Maurice, darling?' in a really sexy voice."

"And?"

"Then he'll sound confused and then you say, 'I'm looking for Maurice Meany. What about that date you promised?' Something like that. Then you hang up."

I was giggling, but I was scared, too. "What if he knows it's me?"

"How can he? Make your voice sound old and sexy. It will be great. He'll be wondering all night who called."

"Here, I'm dialing," Lexie said. She handed me the receiver. The phone rang. Let him not be there, I prayed.

"Hello?" It was him. My throat was so tight I didn't think any sound would come out.

"Hello, Maurice?" It came out as a squeak, and not sexy at all.

"Say *darling*," Samantha whispered.

"Maurice, darling," I echoed.

After a second I slammed down the phone.

"What? What did he say?" the others demanded.

"He said, 'Yes?'" I yelled.

We looked at each other in horror mixed with delight.

"Mr. Meany's first name is really Maurice?" Kaitlin asked.

"It can't be," Lexie said.

"It is. He answered me," I said.

"I can't believe it. We've discovered Mr. Meany's name. Another dark secret to hold over him," Lexie said excitedly.

"I just hope he didn't recognize my voice," I said. "Did I sound like me?"

"I'm sure he didn't, Em," Kaitlin said.

"Let's go back to my room," I said. "I think my nerves have had enough phone calling for one evening."

We were heading to the door when the phone rang. We all jumped a mile.

"It might be my mother calling to check on us," I said. I picked it up.

"This is the telephone company," a woman's voice

said. "We've just had a complaint about a crank call and we've traced the call to this number . . ."

My heart did flip-flops. "They've traced the call," I whispered, holding my hand over the phone. "Mr. Meany must have called up and complained. What am I going to do? Now he'll know it's me and he'll think I'm totally stupid. He'll know I have a crush on him. I'm doomed."

Worse and worse thoughts started creeping into my mind. "You don't think the phone company sends out the police when they get a complaint, do you? Oh, my gosh, Lexie, tell me what to say now!"

I tried to hand her the receiver. She pushed it away. "Don't ask me," Lexie shrieked. "Pretend they've got the wrong number. Say nobody's home and you're the answering machine . . ."

Suddenly there was a burst of laughter outside the door. Kaitlin, who was nearest, pulled it open. Samantha was standing there, holding my mother's cordless phone from her office. "Gotcha," she said sweetly.

"You should see your faces," she spluttered as we stared at her blankly. "Boy, was that ever terrific!"

"It was you," I yelled, slamming down the phone. "You pretended to be the phone company! You called on my mother's business number."

She nodded, still laughing too hard to talk. "And you bought it."

"It wasn't funny," I yelled. "You nearly made my heart stop. I thought I was going to be in big trouble. I thought Mr. Meany was going to think I was a total dweeb."

"I thought it was pretty funny," Samantha said.

"It was a really mean thing to do," I yelled. "I thought we were going to be friends."

"We *are* friends," Samantha said. "It was just a joke."

"You scared the daylights out of me."

"Sorry. I just couldn't resist," she said, still laughing. "It was so easy." She paused and looked at my furious, bright red face. "Think of it this way, Emily. At least you know that Mr. Meany hasn't really traced your call."

I turned away, staring blindly out the window.

"It was pretty funny, Em," Lexie said gently. "And pretty clever, too. It really made us freak out."

"And I'd say that made us even for tonight, wouldn't you?" Samantha went on. "One mud bath against one phone call."

"I guess so," I said slowly. "Okay, so it was pretty clever. You really got me worried there. You sounded so grown up."

"Yeah, people say my voice sounds really old on the phone," Samantha agreed.

"Let's get out of here," I said, "before Meany really does decide to complain about us. I'm through with crank calls, thank you."

I pushed the others out of the room.

"You guys want to watch TV or what?" Lexie asked.

"We could work on your skit," Samantha said.

"You said it was stupid and babyish," I accused.

She shrugged. "It is. I'm not being mean. I'm just thinking what seventh and eighth graders will say if they have to watch a silly Christmas story."

"She could be right, Emily," Kaitlin said.

"So what are we going to do?" I asked. "We

told Mrs. Bliese we'd come up with something."

"I know," Samantha said. "Why don't we do a rap? I'm great at rhyming. We used to do it all the time."

"But what will it be about?" I asked.

"About the teachers—especially Mr. Meany." Samantha paused, thinking, then she started dancing around. "Listen, how about something like this:

> *Going to tell ya 'bout a guy,*
> *he's fit, he's lean.*
> *He's bad, he's cute,*
> *but he's also mean.*
> *M-M-M-Mr. Meany!"*

We leaped up, clapping and cheering. "That was great. Let's do some more," we yelled.

Lexie jumped up, waving her arms. "How about this?

> *When he makes me run the Monday Mile,*
> *I don't have the strength to smile.*
> *Mr. Meany . . . M-M-M-Mr. Meany."*

Kaitlin joined in:

> *"I could be the queen,*
> *If it weren't for Mr. Mean.*
> *M-M-M-Mr. Meany."*

We started adding lines about all the other teachers. We were really cooking now, yelling and laughing incredibly loudly.

"And we finish with something like this," Samantha shouted. *"Watch out for this guy, that's what I said, If you make it through his class, you're either fit or you're dead."*

We all froze as the phone rang in the next room.

"It's him!" I yelled.

"Relax," Samantha said. "It's probably your mom. I'll get it if you like."

She ran to pick up the phone. We came in just in time to see her demanding, "Who is this?"

Then she got very red and slammed down the receiver.

"Who was it?" we asked.

"It was a crank call," she said, "but I can guess who it was. That big tub of lard, Pee Wee. He's been saying dumb things to me ever since I got here. You know, stupid, childish jokes about my figure. It is so embarrassing. I mean, I can't help how I look, can I?"

I had never thought before that Samantha might be embarrassed about looking so grown up. I thought she liked looking that way. In fact, I thought she tried to look grown up.

"You don't know how hard it is when you're the first person in the class who has to wear a bra," she said. "Everybody makes dumb jokes all the time. I hate it."

"Pee Wee is always making dumb jokes about all of us," I said. "Especially me. He's always teased me. All my life."

"Then maybe it's time he stopped," Samantha said.

"Huh. How are you going to stop him?"

A wicked smile spread across her face. "It worked with you, didn't it?"

"Samantha!" I exclaimed. "You're not thinking of calling him and pretending to be the phone company, are you?"

"Why not?" she asked. "It might scare him enough that he'll never think of teasing you again."

"It might work, Em," Kaitlin said.

"And even if it didn't stop him from teasing you forever," Lexie said, "I'll bet it would give him a terrible scare."

"Yeah!" I said. "I'll bet it would. It sure scared me. Okay, Samantha, do it!"

"What's his number?" she asked.

Lexie thumbed through the phone book. "Here," she said. "Start dialing."

We stood around Samantha, all holding our breath. We could hear the phone ringing at the other end. Then we heard a deep voice say, "Hello."

"Good evening, sir," Samantha said in her smooth, grown-up voice. "This is the phone company and we are following up on a complaint we've just received about a crank call, made from your number . . ."

We heard a muffled voice coming through the line and we watched Samantha's eyes open wide. Then she said, "This is just a warning. But make sure he doesn't do it again."

She hung up and dissolved into laughter. "That was Pee Wee's dad," she shrieked. "And he said, 'That would have to be my son. Don't worry. He's going to get it.'"

"I don't believe it! It's perfect," Lexie yelled. "Pee Wee Pugh's going to get it."

She grabbed me and swung me around. The other two joined in and we were just waltzing out of my mom's room when the front door opened and Mom and Ed came in. They looked at us in surprise.

"Sounds like you girls have been having a good time," Ed said.

"We've been having a great time," Samantha said. "Right, Em?"

"Right," I said. And you know what? I really, really meant it.

ELEVEN

The next morning we were up early, and of course Lexie and Kaitlin had to go out to play with the animals while my mom made pancakes and sausages for breakfast.

"Go with them, Samantha," Ed said as we three put on boots and headed for the door.

Samantha shook her head. "I'm not exactly into animals," she said, looking down at her glass of juice.

"Then you need to learn if you're going to be part of this family," Ed told her. "They just take some getting used to. I had to learn when I moved in here, didn't I, honey?"

"You sure did," Mom said, laughing. "Ed's the only person who ever got upended by a pygmy goat!"

Samantha and I exchanged a secret grin.

"It just takes a little time and patience, Samantha. But Emily will show you what to do. Go on, go out and get to know the horses."

Samantha shrugged and followed me outside. It was a perfect clear winter day, just crisp enough to be wintery but the sun was already warm on our faces. We didn't bother to put on our jackets.

"Nowhere near the goats, okay?" she muttered.

"The billy is actually very sweet when you get to know him," I said, "but we can take it slowly."

Lexie and Kaitlin were already squatting down, petting our youngest foals through the fence. I went over to join them. Samantha still hung back and I wondered if she was being snobby again.

"Don't you want to come pet them, too?" I called to her.

"Okay, I guess," she said. She came across and squatted down beside me. "They are kind of cute," she admitted as one tottered over to her on spindly legs. "It's just that I've never been around animals. I don't know what to do. Do they bite or anything?"

"Just don't make any sudden moves to startle them, and you'll be fine," I said. "Look, like this."

I gently stroked the side of the nearest foal's neck. Samantha did the same. "It's so soft," she said. "We never had any pets. My mom's allergic to hair and fur and all that stuff."

"You can have pets without hair," Lexie said. "I have a snake and an iguana and a tortoise. They make great pets, right, Em?"

"Uh, sure," I said. To tell the truth I was always kind of scared of her snake and iguana.

"You should get a reptile," Lexie said.

"Uh, thanks but no thanks," Samantha said hurriedly. "You should see the size apartment we live in. There's just enough room for my mom and her clothes. I'm the only pet she has space for." We all laughed but I thought Samantha looked a little sad, too, as we walked back to the house.

After breakfast, Kaitlin's dad arrived to drive her and Lexie home. "So what do you want to do today, ladies?" Ed asked, putting an arm around our shoulders. "Any big plans?"

I looked at Samantha. "Nothing except working on our rap, but we should really wait for the others to do that."

"It's too nice to stay indoors," Ed said. "How about we all go horseback riding?"

"Horseback riding?" Samantha and I said at the same moment.

"When did you ever know anything about horseback riding?" Samantha demanded of her dad.

"Never, but it's about time I learned," Ed said with a grin across at my mom. "Someone around here has been nagging me to take lessons. And I think it would kind of a fun activity for today, don't you?" He turned to me. "You used to ride a lot, right, Emily?"

"All the time," I said.

"And I'll bet you've never had the chance to try it yet, Samantha?"

"No, and I'm not sure I want to. Horses are big."

"You'll love it," Ed said. "It's a real country thing to do. You can tell your friends about it when you go home."

"But I don't know how to ride." Samantha looked panicky. "What if I fall off?"

"Relax, honey. We're just going to start with a trail ride," Ed said. "Just an easy walk. I'm not too anxious to fall off either, remember. It might be too tame for an expert like Emily, but . . ."

"Oh, no. I'd do anything to get to ride again," I assured him.

"Good. I'll go call the stable and see if they've got room for us on one of their rides today," Ed said.

A few minutes later he came back to say he'd signed us up for the two o'clock ride. I couldn't believe it. I was actually going riding again. I was so excited I could hardly sit still all the way to the stables. I was excited, but nervous, too. What if I'd forgotten how to ride and I looked like an idiot?

We parked in the stable yard. A group of horses stood tethered to a fence, already saddled up. "Choose your mounts," the groom said, looking up as he checked a saddle strap. "But don't try and mount until I can help you."

"Why don't you pick for us, Emily?" Ed said. "You're the expert."

My heart was beating fast as I walked toward the row of horses. I had noticed a beautiful chestnut Arabian, not too big but light and elegant. As I came up beside her, she skittered sideways.

"I wouldn't take that one, miss," the stable boy muttered. "She gets spooked easily. A leaf falls on her and she's off like a shot."

I glanced back at Samantha and I remembered what Lexie had said—that I should find Samantha a horse that would run away with her. Then I could save her and be the hero. Of course, that was before Samantha and I became friends. Now I didn't want to get back at her anymore.

Samantha came over to me. "What a pretty horse," she said. "Can I have her?"

"She spooks easily," I said quickly, before I could have any more crazy ideas. "You need a calm and gentle horse for the first ride."

I found her a quiet bay mare and stood beside the groom as he helped her get into the saddle. I thought about taking the chestnut for myself, just to show off. Then I remembered it had been a long time since I had ridden. I might have forgotten how. So I chose a big, surefooted golden palomino who reminded me of Dad's big horse I used to ride.

We started off, on a trail that wound between vineyards. Samantha and I rode side by side. Ed was a little bit behind us. The horses' hooves made soft muffled thumps and there was the smell of wood smoke in the air.

We passed the Christmas tree farm, where people were arriving to cut their own trees. "I've never cut my own Christmas tree," Samantha said.

"We always do," I said. "It's fun. We can never agree on which one is best. Mom always wants a big full tree and Robbie wants the tallest one and I always want to be like Charlie Brown and rescue the little spindly one nobody wants."

We smiled at each other.

"I think I'm going to like it here, Emily," she said quietly.

I nodded.

"It's really nice being part of a family. I've missed that all my life. Before my mom and dad got divorced, he was away a lot and we moved around so much I never made real friends. And since they got the divorce, it's just my mom and me."

"That must be kind of special for you," I said.

She shrugged. "It's okay."

"Living in L.A. and shopping for clothes in Beverly Hills with your mom—that must be neat."

She shrugged again. "The clothes are always for her," she said. "Ever since the divorce she's been Ms. super career woman. She's so busy with her job that she doesn't have time for me. She doesn't even notice I'm around." Her voice caught in her throat. "She didn't even have time to come to my choir performance at school because she was too busy."

"That's tough," I said.

She nodded. "Seeing you guys all together here . . . you don't know what it's like to come home to an empty apartment every day. Until this year I used to go to the after-care program at my elementary school. That was okay, but now I'm too old. They only take you up to eleven. And I don't get to do any after-school activities because there's no one to drive me."

She swallowed hard. "Mom keeps on saying it will get better, but it never will. She'll always put herself first. She always has. That's why they got divorced, I guess."

I was thinking of our noisy kitchen every afternoon and Nana appearing with her latest cake or pie or special dish and everyone helping out when there were chores to be done. It wasn't glamorous or anything, but at least we knew we were a family. I couldn't imagine letting myself into a cold, empty place every day, or eating dinner alone.

"But if you like your dad better, why didn't you choose to live with him?" I asked.

She shook her head. "That's not how it works. She had a better lawyer than he did. Besides, Dad said it was better for a girl to grow up with her mother."

Samantha paused, then glanced shyly at me. "Dad was supposed to get me for the vacations, but Mom's always managed to find an excuse so far. His apartment wasn't suitable before he got married. She always found me a great summer camp or we had to go to my grandparents on the East Coast. My parents have been divorced for three years now and I've hardly ever seen him."

"If you could spend the vacations with us, it wouldn't be so bad," I said. "At least you'd have a family for part of the year. And it won't be long before you're in high school and then you can find lots of stuff to do after school. By then you'll be driving, too."

"That seems so far off," Samantha said.

"Then you should tell your mom how you feel," I suggested. "Maybe she doesn't realize how lonely it is for you and how much you'd like more attention."

"I would if I could get her to stop and talk for a moment."

"Get your dad to talk to her."

"Maybe," she said. "They didn't exactly part on the best of terms. But it's worth a try. I know they've been talking about me. My mom was thinking of sending me to boarding school."

"Boarding school? Do you want that?"

"I don't know," she said. "It might be better than home. At least I'd have kids to do stuff with."

The path narrowed and I let her move ahead of me. As I watched her back I thought how easy it was to be wrong about people. All that bragging about designer clothes and grown-up things was only to hide her loneliness and hurt that her mother had no time for her. If it hadn't been for sleepover and the billy goat, we might have gone through the whole vacation hating each other. I made up my mind to help Samantha have the best Christmas ever.

Ed's big horse lumbered up beside me.

"There's no brake on this thing," he said. "And no gears. I feel very insecure."

"You're doing fine," I said.

"Not when I watch an expert like you," he said. "I can compare the difference between you and Sammy. She's shaking all over the place like a sack of potatoes and you sit there like you're part of the horse."

"I guess I've had a lot of practice," I said.

"We should try and get a horse for you again," he said. "If we can afford it next year."

"Really?" My whole face must have lit up, because he laughed. "Why didn't you ask for one if you wanted one so much?"

I shrugged. "For a long time I always connected horses to my dad. It was too painful to think about riding and to remember he wasn't here anymore."

"You're old enough to go stay with him now, like Samantha is doing," he said. "You shouldn't lose touch. He's probably missing you as much as you're missing him."

"You really missed Samantha, didn't you?"

He nodded. "It almost broke my heart to walk out of her life. Every time I tried to see her, something came up. Either my company shipped me abroad or her mother came up with another wonderful excuse. That's why this visit was so important to me, too."

He coughed nervously. "I want to thank you, Emily, for making an effort with her. I know she's not the easiest person right now. In fact, her mother's having a lot of trouble with her. She's rude and sulky and disobedient at home and she's not fitting in too well at school, either. Her mother is thinking of sending her away to a strict boarding school . . ."

"Send her to a boarding school if you like," I said. "She wouldn't mind that. But not a tough one. She's not a bad person. She's just trying to get attention. Her mother's never there for her—that's the only problem she's got."

Ed nodded. "I'm sure you're right."

"And let her come here for the vacations, so she can learn what a family's like."

"I was hoping you'd say that," he said. He looked at me steadily. "You're a fine kid, Emily. I know I can never replace your dad, but I hope we can be friends someday."

"We already are," I said. "And two dads are better than one. I might even get two allowances, right?"

Ed laughed. "You're too smart for your own good," he said.

We turned from the narrow path and began to walk between two fields. A tractor was plowing, making a *put-put* noise as it went. The lead horses in our group picked up the pace.

"Whoa," Ed called as he was bounced up and down in a trot. "Aren't there any shock absorbers on this thing?"

"Ride into it," I said. "Like this." I showed him how to sit in the saddle and pick up the horse's rhythm.

The chestnut Arabian had moved up beside Samantha. Suddenly there was a noise that sounded like a shot. The tractor we were passing must have backfired. The Arabian neighed, reared, then took off down the path, the rider clinging to her back. To my horror, Samantha's horse followed it. "Help!" Samantha screamed. "Help me! I can't stop!"

I didn't waste a second. I urged my horse forward. I could feel his surprise, but he knew who was boss and he obeyed. His big legs covered the ground quickly as he broke into a gallop. I passed the trail leader. He looked at me nervously. It was obvious he couldn't decide what to do. If he tried to chase us, then all the other horses might try to follow.

Then I was past him, and the bare bushes beside the track were passing me in a blur. I was catching up to them. Luckily Samantha's mare wasn't as fast as my palomino.

"Pull back on the reins," I yelled to Samantha.

"I can't let go of its mane," she yelled back.

I drew my horse nearer until we were racing side

by side. I could see her horse's frightened eyes. I tried to move in closer until I could reach across and grab the reins. Then I pulled like crazy, leaning back in my stirrups. "Whoa!" I yelled. My horse stopped and so did hers. In the distance, I saw that the rider on the Arabian had managed to stop his horse.

The trail boss caught up with us.

"That was some riding, young lady," he said. "I couldn't have done it better myself."

I blushed and managed a smile. My heart was still racing. "I used to ride a lot," I said.

"Anytime you want a job, come over and see me," he said. "I can always use good riders."

"Okay, I will."

He turned to Samantha. "Are you okay?"

She nodded. "I think so. If Emily hadn't caught me, I don't know what would have happened."

"At least you stayed in the saddle," the trail leader said. "We'll make a good rider of you. Get your friend to teach you."

Samantha looked at me with pride. "She's not my friend, she's my sister," she said.

TWELVE

Two weeks later we performed our rap at the school holiday party. All the kids in the audience were clapping in time, laughing at the words and even joining in the chorus.

"M-M-M-Mr. Meany," echoed through the gym.

I was so glad we had followed Samantha's advice and done this rap instead of the Christmas story we'd wanted. Some other sixth graders had done a dweeby performance of *Rudolf the Red-Nosed Reindeer* and it had been very embarrassing for them. Some of the older boys, like Kaitlin's brother, Tom, had almost drowned out the words with their hoots and remarks before the vice principal went over to sit with them. Everyone else was laughing, and it wasn't very nice laughter at all.

Samantha had also helped us work out the dance steps to go with the words. We looked pretty good, all coordinated in our moves. I had wanted to put everyone else in front of me, so they would hide my klutziness. Samantha kept telling me I'd do fine, though. And you know what? I really was doing okay. Not that

I'd ever be the world's greatest dancer or anything. I probably didn't move as well as the others, but I didn't feel like I was dying from embarrassment, which usually happened when people were watching me.

Maybe that was because they'd been treating me like a hero at home ever since I stopped Samantha's runaway horse. And Samantha had told everyone at school, too. We were getting along pretty well and she had even started bugging Mom and Ed about getting me contacts. I won't say we don't fight, but then what two sisters get along all the time?

As Lexie and Kaitlin had thought, it was kind of nice to have a sister. It was fun to lie in our beds and talk at night just before we went to sleep. I also enjoyed listening to her tapes. It was just like having a permanent sleepover.

At school, she was still friendly with Cindy Crawley, but that was okay with me. Just because she was my sister didn't mean she couldn't have her own friends. And Pee Wee Pugh was staying away from both of us! He even blushed when we passed him in the halls.

The rap number ended with the audience screaming and cheering. As we leaped down from the stage, red faced with all that effort, the first person we bumped into was Mr. Meany himself.

"Nice rap, girls," he said, grinning at our total embarrassment. "Very energetic, too. Aren't you amazed at all the stamina you have now? I told you hard work would pay off."

"I hope you're not mad, Mr. Meany," Kaitlin said. "We didn't mean to be rude."

Mr. Meany laughed. "No offense meant and none taken. Actually I was flattered that I'd finally made the Top Forty. But I can tell you girls don't need any more aerobics after this."

"Seriously?" Lexie asked.

He shook his head. "You have all the moves down pat."

"All *right*," Lexie said, and actually gave Mr. Meany a high-five.

"So when we come back after vacation," Mr. Meany went on, "we'll be doing cross-country running. Lots of steep hills, mud everywhere. You're going to love it."

He grinned again and pushed his way through the crowd.

"It's not fair." Lexie sighed. "We'll never get even with that man. Never."

"Just you wait," Samantha said. "You've got me now—at least around vacation times—and four heads are definitely better than three!"

We linked arms and laughed as we made our way through the still cheering crowd.

Here are some great things to do at your next sleepover:

YUMMY TACOS

You'll need:
- 1 lb. ground beef
- 12 taco shells
- lettuce, chopped
- tomato, diced
- white cheddar cheese, grated
- onions, diced
- chili powder or taco mix that comes in the box of taco shells
- skillet or large pan

1) Ask a parent or adult to help you cook. Cook the ground beef and onions in a large skillet until the meat is brown.
2) Carefully drain grease.
3) Place the taco shells on a plate and fill with the beef.
4) You and your friends can then add lettuce, tomatoes and cheese to your tacos. Dig in!

FUN SECRET SLEEPOVER GAMES
TO PLAY WITH FRIENDS

SLAM BOOK

1) Give each girl her own notebook and have her put her name on the inside cover and reserve a page for the following categories:

Most talkative
Best dancer
Biggest flirt
Best athlete
Most talented
Smartest
Cutest
Messiest
Neatest
Most conceited
Best dressed
Most loyal friend
Funniest
Most popular
Most likely to marry first
Most likely to have six kids
Most likely to be a movie star
Most likely to be president

2) Fold over the page so no one can see what you are writing.
3) Pass around the books and have everyone fill in their choice for each category in each notebook.

4) When all the notebooks have been written in, return them to their owners.
5) Let everyone look in their notebooks and see who the winners are in each category.
6) Remember, these are your friends. Leave out categories that might hurt people's feelings.
7) Write in pen so no one can change any answers!

WHAT'S IN YOUR FUTURE? ?

*This is a fun game to help you find out
what's in your future, or at least get you laughing.*

1) On the top of a blank piece of paper, write out M A S H for the kind of house you'll live in. M for mansion, A for apartment, S for shack, and H for house.
2) To the right put four numbers. This will be how many children your friend will have.
3) On the bottom ask a friend for four cities or states she would like to live in. For example: New York, Hawaii, London, San Francisco.
4) To the left ask your friend for four names of boys she knows.
5) Have your friend close her eyes while you draw a spiral in the middle of the page. She should call out when she wants you to stop.
6) Count the rings of the spiral. That is your number.
7) Using that number, go around to all your choices and cross off the ones you land on.

8) Keep crossing out every choice you land on until you have one choice left in each category. That will be what kind of place she'll live in, how many children she'll have, where she'll live, and who she'll marry.
9) Give everyone a chance to play!

TRUE OR FALSE

1) Each person takes a turn telling an event that may or may not have happened to her or someone she knows. If it's true, use a story that you have never told to anyone in the room. If it's made up, make sure it sounds pretty real.
2) After you tell the story, everyone has to guess whether the story is true or made up.
3) Give them a point for each right answer. If you succeed in tricking them, you get a point, too.
4) Go around the circle until everyone has a chance. The person with the most points wins!

THE SLEEPOVER SHOW

1) Before the sleepover, go to a local library and find a play or movie script that has about the same number of characters you'll have at your sleepover. You might even try writing your own!
2) At the sleepover hand out copies of the script and practice acting out the parts.

3) See what costumes and props you can get together.
4) Hold a performance for your family, or plan to
perform the play at the next talent show at
school.
5) If someone in your family has a video camera, ask
them to tape your dramatic performance. You and
your friends can have a great time watching yourselves afterward!

About the Author

Janet Quin-Harkin has written over fifty books for teenagers, including the best-seller *Ten-Boy Summer*. She is the author of the *Friends* series, the *Heartbreak Café* series, the *Senior Year* series, and *The Boyfriend Club* series. She has also written several romances.

Ms. Quin-Harkin lives with her husband in San Rafael, California. She has four children. In addition to writing books, she teaches creative writing at a nearby college.

Don't miss
Kaitlin, Emily, and Lexie's
next adventure in

TGIF! #4

FOREVER FRIDAY
(Coming in December 1995)

Sleepovers are fun, but not when they last forever. Kaitlin, Emily, and Lexie can't wait to get away for a weekend at Lexie's dad's mountain cabin. But by the end of the weekend they can't wait to get away from one another! After a blizzard hits, the girls are trapped in their cabin. Soon they run out of food, firewood and patience. Even if they manage to make it through the weekend, will their friendship survive the longest and coldest sleepover ever?

Coming soon:
TGIF! #5 TOE-SHOE TROUBLE